The Essence of Glow
By Sage Sinclair

PublishAmerica
Baltimore

ISBN: 1-4241-9670-1
PUBLISHED BY PUBLISHAMERICA, LLLP
www.publishamerica.com
Baltimore

Printed in the United States of America

I dedicate this book in memory of a lost son, brother and friend —
LARREN DALE SEITER, JR.
Ride on, my boy!

I would like to acknowledge—
My wonderful husband for his perfect love and his kind ways.
All of my seven children. My sister, Missy. My Uncle Mike.
A special thank you to my dear friend Susan for helping me
make my dream a reality.
Love to all of you!

Chapter One

It was a warm summer day. Emma was eleven years old and on her way to town. A river ran along the edge of the village she lived in. She stopped to poke at a frog with the stick she had picked up. The trip to the market would be a long one, but she would make it exciting and eventful. Emma's mother had sent her to the market with the intentions to purchase some flour. She told Emma that it would be needed right away, in order to have it on time. Her mother knew that Emma's imagination would take her places and that Emma would be distracted from the path she was to take. Emma took her boots off and dipped her toes into the water. It felt warm; she wanted to jump in, but she remembered that her mother had told her to hurry along. Emma thought that to get her feet wet was like eating a peppermint ball from Mr. Butter's candy jar. She remembered the flour and slipped her boots back on and continued with her journey. She had hoped that enough money would be left to purchase one of those tasty candies that she loved so well.

One of Emma's favorite things to do was to go into town,

there was so many things to do and most of all to smell. The scent of lavender awoke her senses. Her mother had kept a bottle of lavender oil only for special occasions. Her mother would dab it on and leave the house, the scent would linger for hours afterwards.

Emma was a pretty, young girl. She had long dark hair. In the summer months blonde streaks would appear and her cheeks would remain rosy from the sun. She enjoyed being outdoors and was full of life and energy. The other children had a hard time keeping up with her as they played.

Emma knew that town was near she could hear the horses hooves hit the hard dirt street as they trotted along. The village was not a large town but had all the things that were needed. Mr. Butter's mercantile, a mill, a bank, a saloon which Emma was not allowed to go near. A barber shop, a doctor's office and a few other shops as well.

Mama told her that Dr. Finley had helped in her birth. Emma felt important with that piece of information. She had not yet realized that the doctor had delivered all the babies in town.

When Emma reached town, she marched right for the wooden sidewalk. She loved the way her boots clicked as she walked. She could now see the mercantile; it was up the way a bit. She entered the front door just as a woman stood at the counter purchasing fabric. The store had the sweet scent of tobacco as the aroma came from the pipes that two men smoked while they played checkers by the old wood stove that was next to the big window. Emma walked directly to the jar where the peppermint balls were. She visually spotted the largest and smiled as she reached in and retrieved it. Her mouth watered at the thought of the taste. She popped it into her mouth as she tossed it from cheek to cheek with her tongue.

"Mmmm," she said.

She turned to face the counter where Mr. Butter stood as he enjoyed Emma's happiness.

"Well hello, Emma, and how are you today?" he asked.

Emma looked up to him with a grin and said, "Just fine, Mr. Butter."

He giggled at Emma because her mouth was so full of candy he could hardly understand her words.

"How is your family?" he asked.

"Good," she answered.

Emma struggled in her bag to find the money her mother had given her. She handed Mr. Butter the coin and waited for her change.

"Here you are, Emma, four cents," he said.

"Thank you," Emma said as she turned and walked for the door.

Mr. Butter quietly shouted, "Have a nice day."

Emma returned home empty handed. She walked in the door of her home whistling a pretty tune that she had learned from her father. She acted as though she hadn't a care in the world. Her mother caught eye of this.

"Emma May Appleton, what have you been up to and where is my flour?" she shouted. Emma knew that when Mama had her hands on her hips she was in big trouble. Emma's eyes grew as large as the candy in her mouth that she tried so hard to conceal. But that made it more noticeable.

"I'm sorry, Mama, I will go back to the market if you want me to," she said with her southern drawl. Emma watched as her mama stood with her hands rested on her hips.

Emma jumped when her mama suddenly waved one hand and said, "Oh no, you won't. Go get yerself washed up fer supper." Her mother turned so Emma could not see her smile and she said, "I just might have enough flour if I scrape the corners of the tin. Um, may I have my five cents back please?"

Emma reached into her pouch and handed her mother the change that was left. She turned quickly in hopes that her mother wouldn't discover the missing penny.

"Miss Appleton, may I ask where my other penny is?" her mother asked.

Emma quickly turned and said with excitement, "Oh, Mama, I could smell the peppermint before I got into town. It smelled so good I just had to taste one. I started talkin' to Mr. Butter and that's probably when I forgot to think about flour." Then she took a breath and sighed.

Her mother waved her hand as to shew Emma away and turned as she said to herself, "Whatever will I do with that child?"

Even though she only got one biscuit instead of two like usual, supper was still yummy, Emma thought. When she was done eating she put her dirty dishes in the wash bowl. She kissed her mother and joined her father by the fireplace. Every evening he sat in his rocking chair and smoked his pipe.

"Papa, will you play a song for me?" Emma asked.

He nodded his head once, reached for his violin and said, "Anything for my little girl."

By that time her mother had finished in the kitchen and joined them. Emma gazed at her father in admiration. There was no man like her papa, she thought. When he was finished her mother said, "Okay, Emma, I think it's time for bed."

Reluctantly Emma replied, "Okay, Mama." She kissed both of her parents and said, "Good night." She walked slowly as she dragged her feet along. She hid behind the door only to spy on her parents. They talked back and forth to one another and smiled. But Emma could not make out their words. She saw her father tilt his head back and give out a roar of a laugh. Unknowingly her mother had just told him of the conversation that she and Emma had earlier that day about the candy. Emma snickered and quickly covered her mouth, careful not to make a sound. Emma quietly turned and went to her room. She climbed into bed and was off to sleep not too long afterwards.

As the morning sun beamed through her window, Emma

opened her eyes. She stretched her arms up as high as she could and sat up. It was going to be a glorious day and she couldn't wait to get outdoors. She slowly climbed out of her big, soft bed. She ran as fast as her legs would go all the way to the outhouse. As she entered the kitchen, the scent of bacon found her nose. She stopped in her tracks to sniff the air. She walked to her room with her head tilted as she still took in the scent. She got herself dressed and pulled her hair back into a ponytail.

"Good morning, Mama," she said as she walked back into the kitchen.

"Good morning," her mother replied solemnly.

Emma had noticed that somehow her mother had acted differently. She was not herself.

"Breakfast smells good," Emma said cheerfully.

"Hmmm," her mother mumbled.

Emma ate quietly as she kept one eye on her mother. Her mother would stop every now and then to wipe her forehead and to catch her breath. Emma thought that maybe she just wanted to be alone, So she ate quickly as she thought of the things she could do today. When she was finished she hugged her mother's legs and walked to the door as she opened it she said, "I'm gonna go play now, Mama."

"Okay, Emma," she said.

Emma stood for a moment as she waited for more from her mother. Then she shut the door behind her as she is on her way to chase butterflies and play with bugs.

Emma had been playing close to home, when she heard her father's shout from a distance. As she reached closer to the house she could hear the anxiety in her father's voice. He stood in the doorway and shouted, "Emma, your mama has taken ill go fetch Doc Finley right quick. Tell him that she is unconscious."

Emma stood and stared at him in confusion as her father said, "Go."

"Yes, Papa," Emma replied as she turned and started to run towards town. As she entered town she ran straight for Doc Finley's. He rented a room around the side of the post office. The door was large and a dark wood with DOCTOR DAVID FINLEY painted in big bold letters. Without knocking Emma ran in; breathing heavily she said, "Mama is sickly really, really bad. Papa say that she is unconchest and you have to fix her."

"Emma, breathe. why don' you sit and rest while I get my bag," Doc Finley said with a smile. He walked into the other room as Emma sat on a nearby chair. He collected all that was needed and neatly tucked it inside of his big leather bag. He rejoined Emma in the other room as he said, "Okay, Emma, I have all I need to fix your mama."

The small carriage stopped in front of Emma's home as she and Doc Finley jumped out. Emma immediately ran inside, the doctor right behind her.

"Thomas, I must ask you and Emma to wait here until my examination is complete," he said.

Emma and her father waited for what seemed to be hours when the doctor finally made an appearance.

Thomas stood and asked, "Well, Doc?"

"I have given her a thorough examination and she is not sick," Doc answered.

As Thomas thought the worst and had begun to panic he asked, "Is she? She? You know?"

The doctor made a silly grin and said, "Now, now, Thomas, before you jump to any conclusions I really must tell you she's not sick."

Thomas has a confused look on his face as he asked, "Well what then is wrong with her?"

"She is with child," Doc answered.

"What?" Thomas asked.

"Olyvia is going to have a baby!" Doc exclaimed.

Thomas sighs with relief and asked, "May I see her?"

"Yes, but only for a moment. She needs her rest," Doc answered.

Thomas shook the doctor's hand vigorously and said, "Thank you, Doc." He was stricken with happiness and anxiety. He smiled widely and grabbed the doctor's hand and shook it as vigorously as the first time and said, "Thank you so much."

The doctor smiled, retrieved his hand and said, "You may go see your wife now."

With one more shake of the hand Thomas said, "Thank you, Doc, thanks a bundle. You have made me a very happy man."

"You're welcome, Thomas. Now go and see your wife. She's waiting for you," Doc said.

Thomas walked proudly across the room with his head held high as he ran into a chair and knocked it over. He smiled and not breaking his stance or his smile, he sat the chair up right and walked out of the room.

Emma sat still in her chair with her head hung low. She hadn't a clue of how she was to feel, so she remained silent. The doctor looked at her long face and asked, "How about you, young lady? What's your idea of a new baby?"

Emma lifted her head and answered, "I hope I get a brother."

The doctor started to fumble around inside of his bag and retrieved something from it. He opened his hand and a peppermint ball rolled around on his palm. With a smile he said, "Go ahead, take it, I have been saving it for a special occasion and I think this is it. Wouldn't you agree?" Emma quickly snatched it up from his hand and popped into her mouth.

"Thank you," she said.

Doc could barely make out what she said but he replied, "You're welcome."

Thomas returned and said, "Emma, your mother would like to see you now."

"She wants to see me?" Emma asked enthusiastically.

"Yes she wants to see you, try not to get her to excited okay?" he answered.

"Okay, Papa, I do my goodest, I promise," she replied with a smile.

Emma peaked around the door into her mother's room. "Come in, Emma, sit next to me. Let's talk a little," her mother said as she patted the bed with her hand.

Emma ran to her mother and wrapped her arms around her neck and said, "I'm so happy to get a baby brother."

"I can't promise you a boy," she said with a smile.

Emma sat on the bed as she scooted close to her mother. Olyvia placed her hand atop of Emma's and said, "It might be a little hectic around here for a while."

"What do you mean, Mama?" Emma asked.

"I will need help doing some things as my belly swells," she answered.

"Why will your belly swell?" Emma asked.

"Right now it's the baby's home and it needs room to grow until it's time to come to our home," Olyvia answered.

"I'm just happy about my brother," Emma replied. Emma wrapped her arm around her mother's waste to embrace her and said, "I love you, Mama."

Olyvia patted Emma's arm and replied, "I love you too."

Emma crawled under the bedding, kissed her mother's belly and fell asleep.

Months had passed and just as her mother had said, her belly did grow. Emma watched as her parents prepared for the new baby. Mama knitted booties and sewed baby clothes while Papa built a cradle. It was all white or yellow because Mama said, "We don't know what our precious little package will be." Emma had gotten more excited and anxious as the big day approached. Every morning she would rise, kiss her mother's belly and say, "Good morning, little brother." In the evening before she retired she would kiss her parents good night and her mother's belly and say, "Good night, little brother."

Emma came home from playing, and as she entered the house she could hear screams from her mother. She started to run towards her mother's bedroom and her father stepped in front of the door. Emma ran into her father with such force that it knocked her back, right onto her behind. Thomas helped her onto her feet and said, "Emma, you shouldn't be here right now."

"What's wrong with Mama?" she asked.

"It's time," he answered.

"Time for what?" she asked anxiously.

"Time for the baby to come," he answered.

"Why is Mama screaming like that? she asked.

"That's what women do. You best go out to play until it's over, I'll send for you then," he answered.

"But, Papa," she whined.

"Emma, I'm not allowed in there either. Please just be a good girl and go play," her father said politely.

With her head hung low and as she shuffled her feet she walked outside. She wandered around the yard kicking at the dirt and the stones until she found a comfortable place to relax. She sat up against a tree and fell asleep.

"Emma, Emma, come quick," her father shouted.

"What, Papa? What's wrong?" she asked.

"The baby is here," he answered with a smile.

Emma ran past her father right to her mother's room and peaked around the door, the same way she had when her mother first became pregnant.

"Come in, my love," her mother said.

Emma slowly walked in and gently sat on the bed next to her mother.

"Are you better now, Mama?" Emma asked.

"Yes I am," she answered.

"He is so tiny. He is a brother, right, Mama?" Emma asked as he wrapped his delicate, wrinkly hand around her finger. Emma's eyes grew wide with delight.

15

"Yes he is a brother," her mother answered with a smile.

"I just knew he would be. What's his name, Mama?" Emma replied.

Olyvia looked at her husband; as he nodded his head once she said, "We have decided to call him Toby, Toby Lee after your grandpa Appleton."

Emma kissed his itty-bitty fingers and said softly, "Welcome home, Toby. I'm your sister Emma and I will never let not one thing hurt you, I promise."

Four years had passed and Emma was now sixteen. She had kept her promise to protect Toby. When he fell, she picked him up, when he had dirt on him she brushed him off. Emma was never irritated by this; after all he was her little brother and she had to keep him safe.

Chapter Two

It was a night when the moon was full. A ray of light shot through the window as if the sun were rising. Emma lay on the bed next to Toby, humming as he rifted off to sleep. He had been ill for the most part of winter. Emma was happy to see summer blossoms. The warm sun would do him good. But he had not recovered as quickly as she had hoped. Emma was at a loss. She could not understand why he had remained such a sickly little boy when she had been so careful in his care. He had fallen asleep, so Emma turned to her side and carefully placed her arm over him. She closed her eyes to rest her tired mind. She silently wished that Toby would recharge and attain his spirit once again. repeatedly she wished for him to be well. Sleep was just around the corner for her when she suddenly felt a tingling sensation in her hand. She tried to resituate it, but that didn't work. She shook it a bit; that also hadn't given any relief. She lifted her arm from Toby's sleeping body and placed along her side, but the tingling remained. She opened her eyes to examine her hand as she brought it close to her face. Her eyes struggled with disbelief at what had been unveiled before her. The sight of her hand displayed something that could not be explained. Her eyes were not deceiving her. The palm of her hand was aglow. It was a beautiful color of blue; it was as if the moon's light had been injected into her hand. What was the presence of this beauty? What did it mean? Emma sat up and tried to grasp the image that laid upon her palm. She was confused and frightened. But she thought that it just couldn't be anything unpleasant. She turned her hand from side to side admiring what was obviously a gift. Then it came to her, the last thought she had before it started was that she wished Toby well. She placed her hand upon his little, sleeping body and repeated the words, "I wish you good health, I wish you good health, I wish you good health." As she became voiceless and the glow was satisfied, it slowly faded away. When all was finished she brought her hand to her face to examine it once more. She smiled, kissed her brother on the forehead and whispered, "I love you." She carefully laid her head next to his and gazed at the moon's light. It seemed to be more vibrant than she had ever seen before. This put quite a crimp on Emma's belief's. Maybe when she woke in the morning it would all be just a silly dream, she thought. "After all things like that just don't happen. Do they?" she asked herself. Emma closed her eyes and sleep was soon hers.

The morning sun woke Emma as it flooded the room with brightness and warmth. She opened her eyes as she stretched to find that Toby was not there. That put a smile on her face. She pulled the bedding up and rolled over to go back to sleep. She suddenly realized that Toby never got up this early before. She jumped out of bed and ran to the kitchen where her mother was cleaning up the morning dishes.

"Mama, where is Toby?" she asked frantically.

"Oh my, Emma, what is wrong? He is only outdoors playing," she replied.

Emma's eyes widened as she asked, "Did he seem alright to you?"

"He's been up for hours, he's been cheerful and full of energy. I thought he wasn't feeling well last. But yes he is fine, why?" she replied.

Emma could not hold this secret of hers in she just had to tell someone. With a surprising burst she shouted, "I made him better."

Her mother stood silent for a moment. She turned her head to face Emma and said with a smile, "Oh I'm sure that your imagination is inventing things. Why don't you go get dressed for breakfast?"

Her reaction was not what Emma had expected. "Mama, you have to believe me. There is something in my hand. My palm turned blue last night it looked just like the moon was in it," Emma shouted.

"Go get ready for breakfast and don't worry about all that right now," her mother said.

"Mama, you do believe me, don't you?" Emma asked quietly.

"Yes, Emma, I believe you now would you please get ready for breakfast?" her mother replied softly.

Emma turned and did what her mother requested. When she returned she ate her breakfast silently and tried to figure out when the blue glow would manifest again. Emma quickly dismissed the thought, gulped her food down and went outdoors to find Toby.

She had hoped to find him in their secret place. They had gone there many times. It was only to be shared by the two of them. They had made an oath that whenever one had a dilemma that person would blow a kiss to the wind, go to the secret place for the other to find and help resolve the problem. They had also enjoyed each other's company. Emma had first taken Toby there when he could barely walk and she would tell him tales of faraway lands. She taught him how to chase butterflies, how to play with bugs, how to poke at the frogs with sticks and how to hide from Mama when she was angry.

Whether he meant to get into trouble or not. Papa on the other hand was not so easy to outrun. So she told him to just give in to Papa. Sometimes Mama would send him to do her work. Just so she could stand and laugh while she watched him chase Emma around the yard as he tried to catch her. Mama gave Emma castor oil for punishment. Emma didn't like that method of discipline and was very angry at Mama, so she poured the remaining portion of the liquid into the cow's oats. Papa had a big surprise when he milked her the next morning. He came into the house covered in manure. He was so angered that he sold her to the butcher the next day. He told Mama, "That she was a no good for nothing cow." Emma never told Mama what happened to the castor oil. But Emma was pretty sure that she figured it out.

Emma finally reached her destination. Toby jumped into her arms and wrapped himself around her.

"Look Emma I'm all better. You made me all better," Toby said.

Emma's reaction was slow, she had thought that he was oblivious through the whole ordeal. How could his memory be so sharp? She just wanted to forget the whole thing. He was happy and cheerful and that hadn't been enjoyed in very long time. It made her heart sing to see him play as a normal little boy so she decided to take advantage of it.

"Well hi there little brother I sure am glad to see you are up so early this morning," she said.

"I'm okay," he said as he jumped from Emma's arms and threw his own into the air.

"Oh yea?" she asked as she bent down and began to tickle him.

"Catch me, sister," he said as he began to run.

Emma ran after him. They chased butterflies, played with frogs, they picked where they had left off before Toby became ill. When the sun began to set they knew that it was time to return home. As they walked Toby slipped his hand into

Emma's and said, "Sister, you don't have to sleep close to me tonight cuz I'm better now."

Emma was a bit overwhelmed by that remark but also happy that he was not ill. She was also a little torn that he didn't need her by him as he usually had before.

"Are you sure?" she asked.

"Yes, sister, I be alright," he said with a smile.

"If that's what you want, little brother," she said

Several months had passed by and Emma hadn't observed anything out of the ordinary. Toby was still in good health. She hadn't spoke with her mother about the night she had witnessed her gift as it came to surface. Emma went for a stroll to get her thoughts in order. As she walked by the water she noticed a duckling that was having a difficult time moving about. She gently scooped it up from the long grass into her palm. "What's wrong, little baby, have you lost your mommy?" she said. She held it for some time, stroking the back of it's head and noticed the strain of trying to move it's wing.

"Oh, little baby, I wish you weren't hurt," she said softly. As Emma spoke these words her palm began to tingle and illuminate as it had before in Toby's room. She watched as the duckling wiggled about and her hand became normal again. She bent down and placed it in the water and watched as it swam away. Emma was puzzled by what had occurred once again and she just had to tell someone of her secret. She sat to ponder for a while but who would understand? She looked up to the blue sky and said, "I don't know who is listening but please tell me what I'm to do with the changes in my hand." At that moment a strong wind blew through the tops of the tree's. The scent of lavender found her nose and her nostrils flared from the wonderful aroma. Emma laid back in the tall grass and closed her eyes to take in the scent that she enjoyed so well.

What is this place? It is so pleasing to the eyes and to the senses.

This quaint little cottage with moss growing on the roof, a chimney so tall it can almost touch the trees. Flowers lined the path up to the front door. Flowers grew everywhere she looked. The sweet scent of lavender was in the air. It was wonderful, tranquil and so peaceful. So much undisturbed beauty. Emma's mind was at ease and she never wanted to leave.

Emma opened her eyes as she felt a drop of rain touch her face as she said, "It was all a dream."

She picked herself up from the ground and began to walk home. Every thought imaginable echoed in her mind.

Emma entered her home and saw that her mother sat at the kitchen table as she mended some garments and sipped on a cup of coffee. By that time the rain had started to fall a little heavier. Emma loved the rain. She had found it soothing and hoped it would help ease the flutter that was deep in her stomach.

"You look bothered, my love. Can I help you with something?" she asked.

"I have a secret, Mama, and it's a big one," she answered.

Olyvia laid the garments back in her basket, pulled her chair close to the table and said, "This sounds important."

"A couple of months ago I told you what happened in Toby's room. Remember it was the night of the full moon?" she asked.

Her mother nodded and said, "Yes."

"Mama, that night my hand had a light in it, a blue light. It never came back until today. When I was down by the water, I picked up this little baby duck. It had a broken wing and when I was holding it in my hand, it started with the light again and the baby swam away after that. What's wrong with me, Mama?" Emma asked.

When she was done speaking her mother sat in silence. She took a sip of coffee and smiled lovingly. She took Emma's hands into her own and said, "There is nothing wrong with you, my sweet daughter. Now you have to listen very carefully to what I'm about to tell you."

Emma sat patiently; her stomach began to flutter more and her hands started to tremble. Her mother spoke softly as she said, "Every woman in our family is born with some sort of gift. You obviously have the gift to heal. Mine is the gift of sight. Which means that I can see things and people and what they might do. You aid the ill to get well again. The first full moon after your sixteenth birthday, is the time your special gift that you are so blessed with, will make itself known. You must keep it to yourself."

"Does that mean that it is bad to have this gift?" Emma asked.

"No, your gift is not bad. Some people fear what they do not understand. They close their minds and then don't realize how special it really is. That is why it is so important for you to keep it hidden. We have grandmothers that did not use their gift wisely and were banished from their village. You have to learn how to use yours in a discreet way or they will break you down." Olyvia replied.

"But, Mama, if it is such a special gift shouldn't we use it to help people?" Emma asked.

"No, people will abuse it in every way they can. Especially if it were to go wrong, because you were asked to do something that was not proper and would be ridiculed. Emma, you are a woman now, please by all means use this gift wisely. As time passes you will learn to control it in a more manageable way. At times you may wish you never had it. The Fox women sometimes tend to yearn for attention and it has gotten us into very difficult ordeals, that in turn were not easily escaped. After that some of us believed it was a curse. Which means that they were careless and indiscreet. That's when the problems became horrible and unfixable," her mother answered with a smile.

"So I do not use it where I will be seen and very careful when I do use it, right?" Emma asked.

Olyvia placed her hand on Emma's cheek and said, "Emma, my love, you are a special person, even without this gift. Just be yourself and everything will work itself out. But you have to promise me that this will be our little secret, a secret between two women."

"I promise, Mama. A secret between two women," Emma said as a smile outlined her face.

"Yes your father knows of our gift. but we do not discuss it unless it needs discussing," Olyvia replied.

"But, Mama, I want to help people," Emma said.

Olyvia removed her hand from Emma's face and gripped her hand tightly as she said in a stern tone, "You must never tell anyone of our secret or see what you are capable of doing. Please tell me that you understand!"

Emma's eyes welled with tears as she said, "I will be careful, just don't be mad at me."

Olyvia loosened her grip, she patted Emma's hand and said, "I believe in you, my love, and you could never disappoint me."

"Thank you, Mama, I feel a little bit better but I'm still scared of what is inside my body. Will that feeling ever go away?" Emma asked.

"As you get older and you decide what direction your taking in life, the feelings will settle. Then you can go with your everyday living. Remember that this is a gift, a blessing. You won't go wrong if you use it wisely. As a woman it is your responsibility to keep your tasks in order," her mother replied.

"What if I get careless and get caught?" Emma asked.

"Is that really a chance you want to take?" her mother replied.

"No, Mama, but there's always a chance," Emma said.

"Well if you are careless enough to get caught then you have to render the consequences," her mother answered.

"I just don't want to hurt anyone," Emma said.

"The only person you will hurt is yourself, but only if you are not careful with your offerings," her mother replied.

"I will be cautious then, Mama," Emma said.

"Well then since we have had our woman to woman talk, I best be fixin' supper," her mother replied.

"Thank you for helping me to understand my gift, Mama," Emma said.

"Just believe in yourself and accept who you are. Now go and let me fix supper," her mother said jokingly as she stood.

"I love you, Mama," Emma said.

"I love you too," her mother replied with a smile.

Emma turned to walk away. "Emma?" her mother asked.

Emma turned to face her and answered, "Yes, Mama."

"You are going to be just fine," her mother said with a loving smile. Emma returned the smile and walked away. As Emma left the room Olyvia thought to herself, *It will work itself out, hopefully.*

Chapter Three

Emma lay silently on her bed absorbing all that she and her mother had discussed. One thing repeated itself in her mind, "You're a woman now, Emma," her mother had said. "But what do women do? They get married and have babies — yuck! None of that sounded good," she thought. Emma decided that the next morning she would go into town and investigate, what exactly women do. As she lay in her bed a smile found her while she examined her hand. She turned it from side to side, this gift that she had inherited made her feel special. But the reality of being a woman, that would be more of a struggle.

Emma awoke, stretched her arms as usual and smiled at the thought that yesterday she was simple Emma, today she was a woman. She climbed out of her big bed that Papa had made for her as a little girl. She could not get in or out of the bed because of it's large size. Emma had thought Papa did this on purpose so he would have a reason to tuck her in at night. But she didn't mind; she enjoyed being dependent on him.

After getting herself dressed, Emma walked through the

kitchen without stopping. "Good morning, Mama, good bye, Mama, I'm going into town," she said. Before her mother could speak a word Emma walked out the door.

Emma had always looked forward to her walk into town because of the things she discovered along the way. Today would be different she had no time for games. She hurried along as quickly as possible.

When Emma reached town she walked straight for the sidewalk. As she clicked along she watched how the ladies walked and talked. She mocked them and she even did the hand motions. *This is easy. I can be a woman with no problem at* all, she thought. As she walked with her head high she thought, *It was sophisticated.*

HELP NEEDED WITH HORSES INQUIRE AT BARN is what the sign read on the side of the building. She walked around the side and down the alley to the barn. The scent of hay was in the air and the manure wasn't to awfully strong. As she walked in she saw five stalls on each side. All were empty except one. She walked over to the beautiful red horse and began to pet her. "How are you today, pretty lady?" she asked.

"Yep, that's her name alright, ain't it girl?" the man said as he gave the horse a few pats. He carried horse shoes in one hand and wiped the other on his torn and dirty overalls. He offered his hand to Emma and said, "Dobbs is my name, Richard Dobbs."

"Emma Appleton," she said as they shook hands with one another.

"Lady is skeptic of people. She doesn't let just anyone near her without snipping. But it seems that she has certainly made friends with you," he said with a smile.

"Since she has taken to me then you wouldn't mind hiring me for the barn help you need," Emma said.

"I was actually looking to hire a male. Some of the work could be a bit much for a girl of your size," Mr. Dobbs said.

"I've been raised on a farm so I'm not afraid of a little hard work," Emma said.

"Oh yes, Appleton. I know your pa," Mr. Dobbs said as he rubbed his chin. "Well maybe we can give it a try. But you will have to work like a boy," he said.

"I will, I promise you won't be disappointed," Emma said excitedly.

Mr. Dobbs raised his hand and said, "Now hold on a minute there, little missy. I only pay ten cents a week. You will need to be here every day."

"Okay I will be here," she replied as she offered her hand to shake. "Deal," she said. Emma smiled and gave Lady one more pat.

"You can start on Monday. Be here promptly at 6:00 am. We will work until dusk, will that be to much for you?" Mr. Dobbs asked.

"No, sir, it's not," Emma answered.

"Well okay, I guess it's settled then. I have to be gettin' back to work now. I'll see you Monday morning. They shook hands one more time and Emma said, "Thank you."

"You're welcome," Mr. Dobbs replied.

Emma smiled and as she turned to walk away Mr. Dobbs shouted, "Wear old britches."

"Okay I will," she said as she turned to leave once more.

Mr. Dobbs watched as she walked away and shook his head as he said, "Girls."

Emma was excited to tell someone of her new adventure, so she hurried home. She entered the house to the aroma of biscuits baking. Her mother was busy preparing for lunch and Toby sat at the kitchen table as he drew a picture.

Emma immediately asked, "Mama, guess what?"

"Emma, what did you do?" her mother replied.

"I left this morning and walked to town. I saw a sign that said, help needed with horses inquire at barn," Emma answered.

Her mother watched and listened with curious ears and asked, "And?"

"And, I inquired, so now I will take care of horses. Ain't that nice, Mama?" she blurted out.

Her mother sighed and asked, "Emma, why did you do that?"

"You said that I'm a woman now. I went and did what a woman would do. Did I do something wrong?" Emma asked.

Her mother could not argue with her but she answered, "No, dear, you did nothing wrong. But I hope you know how to tell your papa."

"Oh, Mama, won't you please tell him for me?" she pleaded.

"You're a woman now. You can figure this one out on your own," she replied.

Emma was frightened at the fact she has to tell her father. She asked again, "Mama, please won't you tell Papa for me?"

Olyvia smiled at her daughter and said, "I'm sorry but I can't help you this time. You'll do alright."

Emma lowered her head scuffed her feet and said, "Yes, ma'am," as she left the room.

Everyone was present for lunch except for Emma's father. She was relieved that he stayed in the field because it gave her more time to think of a good pitch. She didn't want to blurt it out at him like she had her mother. Papa was a stubborn; man he always said, "What I say goes."

Emma heard her mother's voice as she called her to supper. Emma had fallen asleep and was quite upset with herself. She had no time to prepare what she was going to say to her father. She moved slowly as she walked toward the kitchen.

"There's my girl. What have you been doing today?" he asked.

She kissed her father on the cheek and answered, "Hi, Papa, not hardly nothin'."

As she sat down, Toby giggled and Emma shot him a dirty look.

"Mama, come sit; eat with us," Thomas said.

"Be patient, Papa," Olyvia replied.

When Olyvia sat down at the table Thomas said, "We are all here, so will you give tonight's blessing son?"

"Thank you for this food and for my mama who cooked it and the secret Emma has. Aaamen! Ow! Sister, that hurts," he said. Emma had kicked his leg under the table.

"It's time to eat, not for horseplay," Thomas said.

Toby giggled and once more Emma kicked him. "Ow! Sisterrr!" he said.

"What seems to be the problem with you two?" Thomas asked.

"Nothin', Papa," Emma answered.

The family had gotten halfway through the meal when Emma had built up enough courage to talk to her father.

"Guess where I went today, Papa?" she asked.

"Well I guess your gonna tell me ain't you?" Thomas replied with a smile as he took a bite of food.

"Well this morning I went for a walk into town," she said.

"Uh-huh," he replied.

"I met Mr. Dobbs, the blacksmith," she said.

"Yes I know who he is, and?" he asked.

"He's a very nice man don't you think?" she replied.

"Come on, girl, I know there's more—get to it," he said.

Emma looked at her mother and she nodded her head with approval, giving her the okay to tell him.

"He gave me a job today. I'm gonna take care of horses. Ain't that exciting papa?" she asked very quickly.

"My daughter ain't gonna shovel shit unless it's in my barn. It just ain't gonna happen," he shouted angrily.

"But, Papa, I start on Monday morning, I get ten cents a week," she said with tear-filled eyes.

He slammed his fist down on the table as he took everyone by surprise. He shouted louder than the time before as he said, "No! I absolutely forbid it!"

"Mama said that I'm a woman now. I will go Monday and work for Mr. Dobbs," Emma replied through a sobbing voice.

Thomas looked at Olyvia with squinted eyes, she only smiled at him.

"As long as you live under my roof you won't go," he said as he tried to frighten Emma.

Emma stood and shouted, "Then I won't live here no more."

"Emma," her mother said shockingly.

"I'm sorry, Mama, but I ain't livin' with this, this crazy man," Emma said.

Thomas was angered by what Emma said. He stood very suddenly and knocked his chair over. Emma jumped back as she looked at her father as tears rolled down her face and said quietly, "I love you, Papa," as she turned and walked away.

Thomas picked up his chair and calmly sat down. He put his elbows on the table and rested his chin on his hands. The room became silent as Emma returned with her overnight bag in her hands. She stood at the door as Toby wrapped himself around her legs. They both cried as Toby said, "No sister, no go."

Emma sat her bag on the floor and bent down to Toby's height and said, "Come here little brother." She wiped the tears from his small, innocent face and said, "Don't cry, it will be okay. We just ain't gonna see each other everyday, that's all. Now you be a good boy and Mama and Papa. I love you," she said as she kissed his forehead and they embraced each other. She picked up her bag and stood as she said, "I'll be at the Butters'." She walked out the door and slammed it behind her.

Thomas looked at Olyvia and asked, "Did it surface?" He stared at Toby and knew that he was listening.

But Olyvia nodded her head and said, "Yes, Thomas, I'm afraid it did." Without another word spoke he stood and walked to his chair. He picked up the pipe that sat on the table next to it and walked outdoors to relax.

"Mama, what's wrong with sister?" Toby asked.

"Nothing is wrong with your sister, now you finish your supper like a good boy," Olyvia said with a smile.

"Yes, ma'am" Toby said.

It began to get dark as Emma walked to town. She was chilled but did not want to stop and dig in her bag for her shawl. She wanted to get to the Butter's as soon as possible. They were a happy couple and always treated her with kindness. She had thought it a little odd they never had invited anyone into their home when they had visitors. But she just knew they would let her stay with them. Emma's thoughts quickly changed to her father. Maybe she could use her gift to make her father think differently. That thought quickly left her mind because she knew that there would never be a way to fix what was wrong. Papa was a stubborn ornery old man, who would never change his ways.

She finally reached town, but the only sounds she heard were coming from the saloon. She heard people laughing, singing to the music being played by a piano and plenty of shouting. It was all very loud and echoed through the streets and between the buildings.

Emma could see the mercantile just up the way. She walked around to the side of the building where she knew they lived. She sat her bag down on the stoop to fix herself. She raised her hand to knock and hesitated for a moment. She took a deep breath and found enough courage as she knocked lightly on the door. She stood frightened as she heard heavy footsteps. The door swung open and Emma tilted her head up to Mr. Butter as he stood there. He was a tall and very round man with hardly any hair left on his head, what he did have left was white.

"Emma Appleton, come right in," Mr. Butter said with a wide smile.

Emma bent down and picked up her bag. Mr. Butter had a peculiar look upon his face when he saw this.

"Here let me help you with that," he said as he took the bag from Emma.

"I'm sorry to barge in on you like this, especially bein' so late and all," Emma said as she walked up the three steps and into the house. Mr. Butter shut the door behind her and Mrs. Butter entered the room. She wiped her hands on her apron as she talked.

"Joseph, who was just knocking at the door?" she asked. She looked at Emma and then noticed Mr. Butter holding her bag. She looked back at Emma and smiled. Emma stood at the door very still, her already bloodshot eyes began to fill with tears.

"Oh dear, child, are you hurt?" she asked as she took one hand into her own and patted it softly with the other.

Emma stood speechless as the tears began to roll down her cheeks.

"I have just the thing to fix you right up. Let's take a stroll into the kitchen," Mrs. Butter said.

Emma did not move.

"Come on, dear, it's okay. Joseph, you can put Emma's bag in the spare bedroom, thank you," she said as she placed her arm under Emma's and led the way into the kitchen.

"Yes, dear," Mr. Butter said as he shook his head.

"Do you like tea? You can rest here if you like" Mrs. Butter replied as she pulled out a chair from the table.

Emma sat down without a word being spoke and watched Mrs. Butter prepare the tea kettle for their drink.

"Would you like something to eat?" Mrs. Butter asked.

"No thank you," Emma answered.

Mrs. Butter sat while the water heated and asked, "Now what brings you here to us at this time of the night?"

Emma began her story and told of the shouting match that she and her father had and of how it broke her heart to see

Toby in that way. Sometime during the conversation Mrs. Butter made their tea and placed a plate of cookies on the table. Mrs. Butter had done so much to make her feel comfortable, she had hoped that the question she was about to ask wouldn't be to much of a shock.

"Mrs. Butter, I have a question that I would like to ask you," Emma said.

"Well okay, dear, ask away," Mrs. Butter replied.

"Well would it be possible for me to stay here with you and Mr. Butter for a while? I would work in your store free of charge to pay for my room and board," Emma asked quickly.

Mrs. Butter patted Emma's hand and smiled while she answered, "Of course you can, dear. You may stay as long as you like but working for us for room and board is not necessary. How could you if you're working at the stables?" she replied.

"Oh thank you, Mrs. Butter. I won't be any trouble at all, I promise." Emma said excitedly.

"You know, Emma, we have an empty room upstairs. Our son would stay in it occasionally when he painted. You can stay there if you like," Mrs. Butter said.

"You have a son? I never knew that. What is his name?" Emma asked.

"His name is Seth, and he stayed indoors a lot as he was growing up," Mrs. Butter answered.

"Where is he now?" Emma asked.

"He is away at college. He is studying to become an attorney, that is an important name for lawyer, ya know?" Mrs. Butter answered.

"Will Mr. Butter mind?" Emma asked.

Mrs. Butter waved her hand as she smiled and said, "That ole goat, he won't mind. It will be nice to have a young person around here again," she answered.

"Since you insist, I'll take it," Emma said.

"It will need a good scrubbin'. No one has been up there in

over a year, and my son ain't the tidiest boy. It just needs a woman's touch," Mrs. Butter said.

"Thank you for all your kindness and understanding," Emma replied.

"Oh your welcome, dear. It has been to quiet for too long and we could use a little excitement around here," Mrs. Butter said with a smile.

Mr. Butter walked into the room he leaned his large structure against the wall and asked, "Can I come in now? Is the girl talk over? Cuz I don't want to interrupt if it ain't safe just yet."

As Mr. Butter inched his way into the kitchen Emma could smell tobacco from the pipe he had been smoking and it made her think of her father. Mrs. Butter spoke and interrupted her thought as she said, "Emma will be staying in the upstairs room for a while."

"I think that's a swell idea. We could really use some young ambition around here," Mr. Butter said.

"You do?" Emma asked with surprise.

"Yes I surely do and it will get ole Mrs. Goat movin'," Mr. Butter answered.

Everyone laughed at Mr. Butter's joke. Mrs. Butter had somehow managed to place a warm bowl of stew and two biscuits in front of Emma. Not to insult Mrs. Butter she ate; her stomach was in knots due to the nights events.

"Now let's prepare you a room down here for the night. It's just down the hall from ours. That way you won't feel scared in a strange room." Mrs. Butter said with a smile.

Mrs. Butter and Emma walked through the livingroom and the first door on the left was closed. Mrs. Butter opened the door and paused as she pointed to the room at the end of the hallway and said, "See, dear, we are right down there."

The two women entered the room, they put fresh bedding on the bed, and prepared the room for the night. Mrs. Butter walked to the door she opened it and paused once again as she said, "Don't worry, dear, your heart will be enlightened soon; it will all work itself out you'll see."

"Thank you for all of your kindness, I do appreciate it," Emma said.

Mrs. Butter flashed a wide smile and said, "You're welcome, now get some rest. You will need your energy to clean that room tomorrow."

They both laughed and Emma said, "Good night."

"Good night, dear," Mrs. Butter said as she shut the door quietly behind her as she left the room.

Emma changed into her nightdress and quickly jumped into bed. As she closed her eyes she thought of Mrs. Butter's last words. How funny that she had said something her mother always said. That was the last reflection of the day as Emma fell fast asleep.

Chapter Four

As Emma opened her eyes, she could smell the aroma of biscuits baking as it swirled about in her room. She jumped out of bed and got herself dressed as quickly as she could. The fragrance had made her mouth water and she could hardly wait to taste the biscuits she had fixed in her mind. She walked into the kitchen where she watched Mrs. Butter as she prepared breakfast.

"Good morning," Emma said.

"Well a good morning to you, I hope that you slept comfortably. Sit down, dear, I've made breakfast," Mrs. Butter cheerfully said.

"It smells yummy," Emma said as she licked her lips. She anxiously awaited biting into one of the biscuits. Mrs. Butter sat the most beautiful plate of food in front of her. Emma's eyes widened with delight and a smile found her face. It was her favorite breakfast. *How did Mrs. Butter know?* she thought. Mrs. Butter made biscuits with gravy, bacon, eggs and a glass of fresh orange juice. Emma was very happy and hungry.

"Mr. Butter and I are going to the Sunday morning service, would you care to join us?" Mrs. Butter asked.

Emma thought for a moment; her family would be there. She would enjoy seeing Toby again. But she wasn't prepared to face her father just yet. Emma graciously declined and said, "No thank you. I think it's best if I get started on the room, if that's alright?"

"If that's your wish. Don't work too hard, dear, after all it is Sunday," Mrs. Butter replied.

Emma giggled and said, "I'll try not to."

Mrs. Butter kissed her on the forehead and said, "We will be back soon, help yourself to whatever it is you need." She walked out of the room. "Goodbye, dear, we will see you at lunch," she shouted from the other room as she stuck a pin in her hat and she shut the door loudly behind her.

Emma was happy to finally be alone. She ate her breakfast as she savored every bite, crumb and morsel. When she had finished, she placed her dishes in the sink and went back to the table to push her chair in. Her stomach was so full by this time that she didn't want to move. *Maybe I shouldn't have gone back for a second helping,* she thought.

Emma walked into the room she had slept in the night before and made the bed. She put all her things back into her overnight bag. When she had finished tidying up the room she shut the door and walked to the kitchen. She found an old cleaning rag and filled a bucket with water as she headed for the upstairs room.

Emma stopped at the bottom of the stairs and gazed as she said to herself, "Well, here goes nuthin'." She almost reached the top when she noticed that one of the steps creaked quite a bit. She walked back down a couple of stairs and walked back up, but this time she walked to the side and she made no noise. *Well that was pretty silly,* she thought. When she had made it to the door she opened it and stared around the room. Quite a bit of dust had accumulated. She knew that it would require quite a bit of cleaning to get the room back in order. The first thing she did was to get some light into the room, she took down the curtains that hung on the window and shook them outside. As she hung them back up she thought, *Plenty of sunshine will find its way in here now.* The bed was soft but as she sat on it dust shot up and she waved her hand in front of her face as she gave a little cough. She sat on the bed and looked around the room. A night table stood next to the bed with a bundle of sheets wrapped in a cloth underneath of it and a lamp on top of it. A desk stood in the corner with a big wooden chair. A chest of drawers with an attached mirror up against one wall. A wood burning stove in the middle of the room. There was another night table that stood on the other side of the bed with a wash basin on top. In the other corner of the room stood an easel with a few paintings on the ledge of it. Emma sat and smiled at this room being hers. She washed all that was washable and had the room smelling fresh and clean. She only had to change the bedding and she would be through. As she started to strip the bed she heard the step squeak and turned to see Mr. Butter standing there.

"It looks very feminine, Emma. You have done quite a nice job getting it all tidy," he said.

"There was quite a bit of dust," Emma replied.

"There is no need to be polite; we haven't been up here in quite some time, so I know it was not a pretty sight," Mr. Butter said. They both giggled as Mr. Butter motioned his hand to her and said, "Come on down and take break; it is time for lunch."

"I just have a few more things to tidy up and I will be down shortly," Emma replied with a smile.

"Don't be long or Mrs. Butter will send me back up here, and I'm no spring chicken," he said.

They both laughed as Emma replied, "I'll not be much longer I promise."

Mr. Butter left the room and walked down the stairs. Emma hadn't been too far behind him while she carried a rolled up bundle of dirty sheets. With her load of dirty laundry she tripped as she walked through the downstairs doorway.

"Joseph quick help that poor girl before she hurts herself," Mrs. Butter exclaimed. Mr. Butter ran to Emma's aid and quickly took the bundle from her.

"How did you carry that down here without falling down the stairs?" Mrs. Butter asked.

As Emma stood and caught her breath she answered with a giggle, "I rightly don't know."

As the three of them sat at the table to eat Emma asked, "Did you see my family at church this morning?"

"Why yes we did," Mrs. Butter answered.

"And Toby, did you see Toby?" Emma asked.

"Yes we saw him," Mrs. Butter answered.

"How was he?" Emma asked.

"He was running and playing with the rest of the children. He is quite the quick whipper snapper if you ask me," Mrs. Butter replied as Emma smiled with happiness.

After lunch Emma went outdoors to the washtub to clean the dirty sheets she removed from the bed upstairs earlier that day. She hung the clean laundry on the line to dry, then she went to her room to retrieve the remaining cleaning supplies. As she gathered all of her things, she noticed the paintings. There were a only a few, so she began to flip through them, the first one was a of a bouquet of flowers in a vase. The second one was of the front of the mercantile. The third one was a small stone cottage with flowers that grew all around it, *But how could that be?* she thought. It was the same cottage she had dreamt about when she fell asleep by the water a few days before. How could this person possibly have seen into her dreams?. She read the signature it was signed WATERS. Who could this be? The Butters had told her this was their son's room. Had they lied? She put the paintings back on the easel, she picked up the water bucket and the other cleaning things and headed down stairs. After she entered the door she discovered that her father was there. He sat in the livingroom chatting with Mr. Butter. Thomas stood when he saw Emma, he held his Sunday hat in front of him. Emma froze in shock where she stood, when he spoke to her.

"Hello, Emma, your mother asked me to come. I want you to stop this nonsense and come home with me right now," her father ordered.

Emma stood in shock as she answered, "No, Papa, I don't want to. The Butter's have treated me real kind like and they gave me my own room."

"Emma, would you please come home?" he asked in a softer voice.

"I'm sorry, Papa, I can't," Emma replied.

"Get your things and come home with me right now. You are still my daughter and you will do as I say," her father shouted loudly.

Emma began to cry as Mr. Butter stood between the two of them and said, "I think that it's time for you to leave now, Thomas."

Thomas walked to the door with his head hung low, he stopped in front of Emma and without looking at her he said, "I apologize for my behavior, I just want you home safely where you belong."

"I love you too, Papa, but I'm happy here," Emma said through tear-filled eyes.

"Come on, Thomas, I'll walk you to the door," Mr. Butter said.

As the two men stood at the door they shook hands as Thomas said, "Thank you for taking care of my little girl."

"You have nothing to worry about when she lives in our home," Mr. Butter replied.

Mr. Butter smiled and he shut the door behind Thomas. He joined the two women in the livingroom where Emma sat on the sofa sobbing as Mrs. Butter tried to console her. Mr. Butter handed Emma the handkerchief from his pocket and said, "Emma, I am sorry for that, I thought your father was concerned about you. So I am sorry."

"It's okay, Mr. Butter, it's not your fault," Emma replied.

Mrs. Butter stood, smiled and happily said, "Let's have a nice cup of tea, dear, it will help you feel better."

Mr. Butter and Emma looked at each other and smiled as they stood and headed for the kitchen. "Mrs. Butter, why do we always have tea after something bad happens?" Emma asked.

Mrs. Butter giggled and asked, "Don't you know, dear?"

Emma shook her head back and forth and answered, "No."

Mrs. Butter stopped placed her hands on her hips and replied, "Why, dear, it's the only way us old goats keep moving." Laughter filled the room as they continued their walk into the kitchen.

The day carried on without any more incidents. After supper Emma told the Butters, "I must get to bed early to make it to the stables on time, so good night."

She headed for the room upstairs. As she walked in she went to the water basin and poured fresh water into it. She undressed herself and threw on her nightdress and splashed her face with the water. Before hopping into bed she sat on the edge and thought for a moment in disbelief, *This is my very own grown-up room.* She slid under the covers she had so perfectly prepared and inhaled the scent of the sheets. She closed her eyes as she took in the lovely scent of lavender.

Emma was restless and found it hard to sleep. The thought of the paintings would not leave her mind. She lit the lantern and walked to the easel. She stood there and stared and placed the cottage painting to the front. She walked back to her bed and sat the lantern on the bedside table. She crawled back into bed and stared at the cottage painting. As she lay there gazing at the painting her eyes became heavy and fell asleep.

Emma awoke refreshed and ready to begin the day with a

new standing on life. She quickly got dressed into her barn clothes and left for the stables.

Emma walked into the barn and straight toward Lady. "Hello, Lady, how are you this morning?" she said as she gave the horse a few pats.

Mr. Dobbs walked up to her and said, "Good morning, little miss. You look as if you are ready to work."

Emma eagerly said, "Yes I am. What do wish for me to do first?"

Mr. Dobbs rubbed the bottom of his chin as if in deep thought and said, "Well—hmmm, I guess you can walk Lady here out to the field and come back to clean her stall. Now we do have the understanding that this is only a trial basis right? I'll keep my eyes on you for about a week and then let you know if you are able to stay on or not."

"Yes I understand," she replied with a smile.

"Well then I will let you get to work," he said as he clapped his hands together and turned to walk away.

Emma led Lady out of the stall and found that the horse walked with a limp. Emma bent down to further investigate and found a deep cut on the horses' leg. Emma stood and looked around the barn to check if anyone could possibly be watching her. There was no one in sight. She bent down and placed her hand on the wound and said, "I wish you good health, I wish you good health, I wish you good health." Emma's hand began with the mysterious glow once again.

Before Emma completed her rite, Mr. Dobbs walked into the barn and with wide eyes watched her with the horse. He was amazed to see what this little girl had done. When she was finished her palm returned to normal and she stood to pat the horse and let her know that she was alright now. Mr. Dobbs walked away so that Emma would not know that he had been witnessing what she had done. Emma walked the horse out to the field and Lady did not limp once, Emma was proud. As Emma released her she ran and frolicked with the rest of the horses.

Later in the day Mr. Dobbs confronted Emma and asked, "Emma, can I talk with you?"

"Sure, Mr. Dobbs," Emma answered.

"Um," he said as he removed his hat and ran his fingers through his greasy hair.

"What is it, Mr. Dobbs?" she asked curiously.

"I have to let you go," he blurted out.

"But it's only my first day," she replied sadly.

"You are a hard worker but I have hired my nephew at a lower rate of pay. I'm truly sorry but this is the way it has to be," he said as his head hung low and he held his hat. He held out his hand to her and as she saw the coins she asked, "What's this?"

"It's your pay," he answered.

Emma gently picked the money from his palm and said, "Thank you."

"I am sorry, Emma, but there is nothing more that I can do," he said.

"Would you like for me to finish the day?" she asked.

"You're a sweet girl, Emma, but there is no need," he answered as he shook her hand and walked away while scratching his head.

Emma stood there alone with tears in her eyes as she tried to fit the pieces together of what had just took place. She closed the door of the stall she had been cleaning and walked home.

Emma felt a little emotional and wanted to throw herself onto her bed and fall asleep as she cried. She stripped her dirty barn clothes off and then noticed that she had fresh water. She washed herself the best she could and slipped on a simple dress with a daisy pattern. She then brushed her hair and pulled it back into a ponytail. The reflection of the cottage in the mirror had caught her eye. She began to walk over to it and she heard a knock at her door.

"Come in," she said.

"Hi there, Emma, Mrs. Butter went to the stables to give

you a lunch plate, and Mr. Dobbs said that he let you go," Mr. Butter said.

"He hired his nephew at a lower rate of pay," Emma replied.

"Are you hungry?" Mr. Butter asked.

"I'm starved, I missed breakfast this morning," Emma answered.

"Mrs. Butter has lunch prepared and waiting and not patiently I might add," he said as they both giggled.

"We best hurry then," Emma replied with a smile.

After lunch Emma helped with the dishes and decided since it was such a lovely day she would take a stroll through town. The birds sang in the tree tops, the sky was blue, and the sun was bright as a warm summer breeze blew around the bottom of her dress.

The thought of Toby had stuck in her mind. She missed him immensely. If only she could see him, but she knew she couldn't because of the falling out she had with her father. She remembered the oath they had made. She blew a kiss to the wind, she just wanted him to know that he was loved by her. As she finished a gust of wind blew through the trees. Emma smiled because she knew he would receive her message.

Her thoughts of Toby made her happy. She remembered she had chased him and he fell to the ground on purpose so she would think that she had won. She remembered their secret place and how she had used her imagination to make up stories for him. She remembered the funny faces he made when they were eating. All of this is what she had missed from home the most.

"Emma? Emma?" Emma turned to see her mother as she smiled at her. "Emma, are you alright?" Olyvia asked.

"Mama," Emma said as they embrace each other.

"I have missed you," her mother said.

"I miss you too, Mama," Emma replied.

They walk arm in arm with one another back toward town.

"I needed a few things from town and here I am with you.

I must say you are beautiful as ever," her mother said as she patted Emma's arm with her free hand. Olyvia fumbled in her pouch and said, "Oh, I want you to have something," as she handed her daughter a peppermint ball.

Emma's face lit up with delight, she plucked it from her mother's hand and popped directly into her mouth as she said, "Thank you, Mama."

Her mother smiled as she watched Emma push the candy back and forth between her cheeks.

"I want to ask you something, Emma," her mother said.

"Yes, Mama," Emma replied.

"You are cautious with the way you use your gift ain't you?" her asked.

"Yes, Mama, I am," she answered.

"Even if you are careful to see that no one is in sight?" her mother asked.

"Yes, Mama, I have not been found out by no one," Emma answered.

"I want to have a piece of mind and know that you are safe," she replied.

"Can we please talk of something else?" Emma asked.

"Alright, my love," she said as she put her arm into Emma's once again.

"How is Toby?" Emma asked.

"Toby is fine he talks of you a lot. He asks of when you are coming home," her mother answered.

"He asks of when you are coming home," her mother answered.

"Well here I am," Emma said as she stopped in front of the mercantile. Olyvia removed the hair from Emma's face and said, "I love you, my beautiful daughter."

"I love you too, Mama," Emma replied.

The two women lightly embrace and Emma walked away slowly and turned once to wave at her mother. Olyvia waved back and smiled as she stood and realized that her daughter had forgot that she has the gift of sight.

Chapter Five

Emma walked into the kitchen to find that Mrs. Butter had been preparing supper. *I must have been lost in my memories for some time,* she thought to herself.

"Did you have a nice stroll, dear? You have been gone for quite some time," Mrs. Butter asked as Emma sat at the table.

"It was relaxing. I had a visit with my mama while I was out and we were able to talk a bit," Emma replied.

"Would you like for me to make you a cup of tea?" Mrs. Butter asked.

Emma giggled and said, "That's quite alright. I am going up stairs to rest awhile before supper."

"Would you like for Mr. Butter to fetch you when supper is ready?" Mrs. Butter asked.

"Yes, thank you," Emma answered as she pushed the chair she sat on under the table. She walked over to Mrs. Butter and kissed her on the cheek.

"I'll see you in a bit," Emma said.

"Okay, dear, you go and have yourself a nice rest," Mrs. Butter replied with a smile.

Once in her soft bed Emma lay as she stared at the cottage painting and thought of who the artist could be. She became lost in thought she tired and fell asleep.

Emma awoke to what seemed to be an overly loud knock at her door.

"Just a moment," she shouted.

She opened the door to find Mr. Butter with a silly grin on his face as he said, "Supper is ready."

"I'll be right down, I would like to freshen up a bit first," she replied.

"Okay I'll tell the missus. Try not to be to long," Mr. Butter said as he stood and smiled at her.

After Mr. Butter left Emma splashed water on her face and quickly straightened her hair as she thought of the grin Mr. Butter held on his face.

Emma could smell the food when she walked in the door. As she walked into the kitchen Mrs. Butter had the table all set. She had made mashed potatoes and gravy, fresh green beans from her garden, biscuits and fried chicken. As Emma sat down she noticed that Mr. Butter still carried a silly grin on his face. As she started to fill her plate she asked him, "Would you please pass me a biscuit."

"Would you like butter on it?" he said jokingly.

Emma looked at him with disbelief and became speechless. She started to laugh as the Butters joined in. Everyone laughed so much they held their stomach to try to keep it from hurting. After a while of laughing Mrs. Butter spoke up and said, "I have a surprise for you, Emma."

"What is it?" Emma asked excitedly.

"Do you know Ruthie Marie?" she replied.

"Ain't she the librarian?" Emma asked with curiosity.

"Yes she is, she was in the store today picking up a few things and had mentioned to me that she would be retiring soon. She also mentioned that she needs to find a stable woman to replace her when she leaves. So I told her about you, and I said that you would make a wonderful librarian. She would like to see you and explain how things are done there. I think you should accept what she offers. It would be a way for you to spread your wings so to speak," Mrs. Butter said as she took a deep breath.

"Oh, Mrs. Butter, thank you. I'll go see her as soon as I can," Emma said happily.

"Emma, do you still want butter for that biscuit?" Mr. Butter asked as he offered her his hand as a butter knife laid on top it. The room filled with laughter as Emma pretended to swipe his hand with the knife and butter her biscuit.

Emma helped clean up the supper dishes. She went to her room and climbed into bed. She had no time stare at the painting; her day had exhausted her. She fell right to sleep when she laid her head on her pillow.

The shadowy figure of a man entered through the door. He walked over to the bed and removed all of his clothes. He sat on the bed yawned and slid under the covers. His nose found the scent of lavender and he thought, *These sheets smell like woman.* The delightful scent relaxed him, he closed his eyes and fell asleep.

Emma opened her eyes to see the cottage painting and this put a smile on her face. She rolled to her back to stretch as she did every morning. When she brought her arms down she felt something in bed next to her. Without looking and unclear of what this was, she felt around with the palm of her hand.

The mystery man lay there not uttering a sound, only revealing a smile upon his face. He wondered what would come next. As Emma felt whiskers she thought, *Oh my sweet cowbell this is a man's face.* She turned her head toward him and he did the same. As they were now eye to eye he smiled at her and said, "Good morning." At that moment Emma began to scream loudly, she jumped out of bed as she covered herself with the bedding. The man jumped out of bed on the other side bearing all as he held his hand up and said, "Calm down, miss, there is no need for that." He then tried to cover himself with the corner of a sheet.

"Who are you? And what the hell are you doing in my room, in my bed?" Emma asked loudly.

"A lady should not have that kind of mouth," he replied calmly, as he juggled to hold the sheet over him and point his finger at Emma.

"Who are you?" she asked almost in a shout.

The door flew open and Mr. Butter came racing in as he shouted, "What's wrong? Are you alright?" As the two men stared at one another they both smiled and embraced, slapping the other's backs.

"Seth, my boy, when did you get in?" Mr. Butter asked.

"Hi, Pop, I slid in late last night," he answered.

"Last night? We slept together all night?" Emma asked with alarm in her voice.

"I see you have met, Emma," Mr. Butter said.

"Yes we have met, but not in a proper way. My name is Seth, Seth Butter," he said as he offered his hand the best he could. They shook, he bowed and kissed Emma's hand while he tried to keep himself covered.

"Emma Appleton," she replied calmly.

Mr. Butter slapped Seth on the back and said, "You best come see your ma."

"Sure, Pop," Seth said.

Mr. Butter turned to walk away and said, "See you at breakfast." As he walked by Emma he looked at her from the corner of his eye and smiled as he said, "Both of you."

As the door shut Seth asked, "Well, miss, may I escort you to breakfast this morning?"

"No you may not, now get out," Emma said rudely as she pointed to the door.

"Do you expect me to go like this?" he asked as he looked down to expose a partially nude body.

"Put your britches on and quick," she said.

Seth stood silently and he stared at her.

"What?" she asked sarcastically.

"Would you mind very much turning your pretty little head?" he replied.

"Yes," she said softly as she turned away and thought to herself how bronzed his body was, how hard his body looked and how well endowed he was. His hair was curly brown and Emma wanted only to run her fingers through it. As she stood there lost in her thoughts she hadn't noticed he had left until she heard the door slam shut behind him. She sat on the edge of the bed and thought of this beautiful man, she tried to make sense of what had just happened.

Emma walked into the kitchen with all the elegance she could as she tripped on a rug. Seth bent down and offered to help her to her feet as he said and tried not to let her see him laugh, "Let me help you."

She walked to the table and Seth pulled her chair out and when she sat he helped push it in. All the while Mr. and Mrs. Butter are watching every move Emma and Seth make, while they sat at the table with a smirk on their face.

"Are you comfortable?" Seth asked.

"Yes, thank you," Emma answered as she situated herself and put her chin to the air.

Mr. and Mrs. Butter pointed their faces back towards their plates as if nothing had been heard from Emma and Seth.

"So, son, what are your plans for the day?" Mr. Butter asked.

"I thought that I would walk around town and review things a bit," he answered.

"It's still the same old hick town it was when you left," Mr. Butter said as everyone but Emma laughed; she was the only one who did not find the joke amusing.

"Did you sleep well, dear?" Mrs. Butter asked.

"Yes, ma," Seth answered.

"I was talking to Emma," Mrs. Butter replied.

"She didn't stir all night," Seth said as he let out a loud laugh.

"Tssk!" Emma said.

"Well I thought it was funny," Seth replied.

"I slept well, at least until I woke up and found a strange man in my bed," Emma replied as she looked at Seth with squinted eyes.

"You were in MY bed," Seth said in an angry tone.

"No, you were in my room and in MY bed," Emma shouted.

"You got that wrong little girl," Seth shouted back to her.

Emma stood with her hands on her hips and shouted loudly in Seth's face, "Who are you calling a little girl?"

"You! Little girl, little girl, little girl!" Seth shouted in her face as he stood with his hands on his hips also.

Mr. Butter sat quietly and watched in amusement and laughed quietly to himself. Mrs. Butter stood pointed her finger at the two young people shaking it vigorously and shouted, "You two sit down right now."

"Jeez, ma, you don't have to yell," Seth said as he sat down in his chair.

Emma and Mrs. Butter sat down also. After collecting herself Mrs. Butter quietly said, "We are all living in the same house and we have to learn to get along. Seth, you can stay in your room down here and Emma can continue to stay in her room upstairs.

Emma looked at Seth nodded her head once and said, "Hmmm."

"But, ma," Seth said as he looked at Emma and stuck his tongue out at her.

Mrs. Butter put her finger to her lips and said, "Shh, just listen."

Seth lowered his head and said, "Yes, ma'am."

"Seth, you used that room only for painting anyway," Mrs. Butter said.

"But, ma," Seth said.

"You best listen to your ma, boy, and make it easy for all of us," Mr. Butter said with a smile as he and Seth laughed. Mrs. Butter joined in while Emma sat quietly and ate. She was frightened on losing her room. She would then be forced to move back home and all her chances of being a woman would diminish.

Seth looked at Emma and asked, "Come on, girl, why ain't you laughing?"

Emma stood as she threw her chair back knocking it over and shouted, "How many times do you have to be told? I'm not a girl!" She stumbled over her chair as she quickly ran from the room.

Seth smiled as he sat the chair upright while he watched her leave the room and said, "She's a feisty one."

"Boy you best leave HER alone," Mrs. Butter said sternly.

"Oh, Amelia, they are only young'uns or have you forgotten that?" Mr. Butter replied.

Mrs. Butter immediately blushed, she waved her hand at her husband and said, "Oh you old goat," they both giggled.

"I'm eating," Seth said as he pretended to eliminate the food he had ate.

Seth strolled through the village as he shook hands and talked with old acquaintances. But he just couldn't remove Emma from his thoughts. Her long, curly, dark hair. Her small slender form, when she became angry he found it hard to keep himself composed. How can this female possess such a grip on him?

Emma walked by the river's edge as she kicked at the rocks and dirt. She tried to skip stones but she found it hard to release her thoughts of Seth. He was tall, handsome and his body is pleasing to the eyes. She just wanted to slide her fingers over his bronzed skin. How could this male possess such a grip on her?

Emma returned to her room some time later to find a

delightful object. *Wherever did this come from and from who?* she thought. She walked slowly around this object and ran her fingers along the edge of it. It was beautiful, heavenly, even. She quickly ran down the stairs and in the door straight into the kitchen. She stood as she tried to catch her breath as Mrs. Butter asked, "What is it, dear?" as she placed her hand on Emma's back.

As Emma had her hand to her chest while she tried to catch up with her breathing she said, "There's a, a bathtub in my room, it's big, it's a big wonderful, beautiful bathtub."

Just then Seth walked into the room concealing the smile he had just possessed and said, "I bought it for you and had it delivered while you were out."

"Why did you buy me such a costly gift?" Emma asked.

"I wanted to do something nice for you. Especially after the adventure we had this morning. Besides if you are going to be staying in my room, I don't want you to be stankin' up the place," Seth answered.

Emma came to the conclusion that in Seth's own way he had tried to be sincere.

"Thank you, Seth, that was very thoughtful," she replied.

"You're welcome, girl, Emma," he said with a smile.

"Come on, dear, and show me this new tub of yours," Mrs. Butter said as the two women head for the door. As they passed by Seth Mrs. Butter whispered in his ear, "You're a good boy, Seth Butter," and winked as she left the room. Seth smiled at his mother's approval.

Mrs. Butter held her hand to her chest as she leaned her body against the frame of the door. Emma turned to notice her as she tried to walk to the bed.

"Let me help you," Emma said as she wrapped her arm around Mrs. Butter's shoulder and walked the rest of the way to the bed with her.

"I must say that is some beautiful tub you have there, Emma. But if you don't mind I must rest on your bed for a bit," she said as she lay down. Emma pulled her feet up for her.

"Thank you, dear. I'm going to close my eyes for a bit, then we will chat about your new tub, okay?" Mrs. Butter replied.

"You take all the time you need," Emma said as she sat on the edge of the bed.

"I only need a bit of time to collect my energy," Mrs. Butter said as she laid her arm over her eyes.

"Do you ever wish you were healthy again?" Emma asked.

"I'll never be fit, I'm too old," Mrs. Butter answered.

"You take all the time you need and when you are ready you will feel much better," Emma replied.

"Whatever you say, dear," Mrs. Butter said with a small giggle.

Emma held her hand over Mrs. Butter's chest and began to say to herself, "I wish you good health, I wish you good health, I wish you good health," Emma's palm began to brighten with the mysterious blue glow. It was not as bright as the other times; Emma believed it was caused by the loss of touch to Mrs. Butter's body. As she sat on the edge of the bed her hand hovered over Mrs. Butter's chest and her breathing became more regular.

Emma turned her head suddenly when she heard the stair squeak and saw Seth as he stood there in awe and watched her. She pulled her hand back immediately and the blue glow faded away. Seth stood in silence as he tried to make sense of what he had just witnessed. He cleared his throat to catch his mother's attention.

Mrs. Butter uncovered her eyes to see Seth and quickly sat up and replied, "This is a real nice tub son, what's that you got there?"

He looked down at what he held in his hand and said, "Uh, here this is for you." As he looked up he gave Emma a square package wrapped in pretty white paper that was held together by a red bow.

Emma accepted the gift and said, "Thank you, what is it?"

"Well if you open it you will find out," Seth replied dryly.

Emma's eyes lit up with delight as she opened her gift to discover lavender oil in a beautiful glass bottle, a bar of lavender soap wrapped in pretty purple paper and a large body sponge.

"This is my favorite scent, how did you know?" she asked as she smiled and sniffed.

"The sheets," he answered.

Emma wrapped her arms around him and said, "Thank you so much."

Seth could feel the heat from her body when she touched him. Her touch was soft and delicate just as her frame was. He wanted her, but he knew that now was not the time for this.

Emma pressed her body next to his and it made her feel warm inside. She was unsure of the feeling she had between her legs. She only knew that she wanted to be with him. She quickly broke the connection between them when she felt odd sensations rise through her body.

"Ooh dear me I must get started on lunch or poor Mr. Butter will fade to nothing," Mrs. Butter said as she laughed at her own joke. She stood from the bed and headed for the door as she said, "Don't you young'uns be long." Seth and Emma laughed as she walked down the stairs.

Emma was frightened that once they were alone Seth would taunt her over what he had seen.

"It suits you," he said.

"What?" she asked.

He pointed to the bathtub and said, "The tub, it's almost as beautiful as you are."

Emma was stunned at his words; she only stared into his dark eyes and said, "What a lovely thing to say. Thank you."

"Well Ma is probably wondering where we are. We should go before Pop melts away," he said as they both laughed.

"We wouldn't want that to happen, now would we?" she replied.

"After you, miss," he said as he rolled his arm about towards the door.

Emma started down the stairs as Seth stood at the door for a moment. He slapped himself in the head and said silently, "What the hell was that? Beautiful as a damn bathtub?" He just shook his head and walked out the door as he shut it behind him.

Chapter Six

Emma introduced herself to the librarian. They discussed how Emma was to perform her duties and the function of the library. Ruthie Marie talked of everything she could think of. Emma smiled, nodded her head and said, "Oh yes," once in awhile to make it seem as if she truly listened. She just couldn't erase her thoughts of Seth from her mind. Emma was suddenly shook from her daze as Ruthie Marie said, "You can start next week, right after I retire." They shook hands, Emma smiled as she said, "Thank you it sounds very exciting. I can hardly wait." She turned to walk away.

"Emma, have you forgot something?" Ruthie Marie asked as she handed Emma a key with a smile.

"I can't be a librarian if I can't get into the library," she replied as she accepted the key and they both laughed gayly.

Emma fell asleep almost instantly as she lay in her bed and gazed at her new tub. Which took her thoughts from the cottage painting.

The morning found Emma smiling as she awoke from her

slumber. The sunshine peeked through the curtains and she knew that it was going to be a glorious day.

"Just a moment," she shouted as she heard a knock at the door. She hopped out of bed in a hurry as she tried to cover herself she fell to the floor with a big thump. Seth stood on the other side of the door with a big grin upon his face he knew what had just happened inside. Emma opened the door with a smile as she tried to collect her composure and breathe normally.

"Good morning," Seth replied as he smiled.

"Good morning," Emma said as she tried not to lose her balance.

"Ma sent me to fetch you for breakfast." Seth replied as he tried not release a laugh.

"I'll be right down," she said with her head turned to one side. She was oblivious to his smile.

"Don't be long, okay?" he replied.

"Yea," she said.

Seth walked down the steps as he laughed and shook his head.

Emma ate her breakfast in a hurry, apologized for not participating in the clean up. Then she quickly shot out the door.

Emma walked the path that ran along the river's edge. She took in the sights and the fragrance of wild flowers. She sat under a tree and closed her eyes to listen to the songs of the birds and the rippling of the river.

"Emma? Emma?" she heard. What man's voice was this? It was so soothing and familiar. She looked up from where she sat and there he stood as dashing as ever. He offered her his hand and said, " Emma my darling ." She placed her hand in his as she stood to face him. "I knew that I would find you here, under our tree," he said. Emma looked into his warm eyes and could see the love he held for her. "Let's walk my darling." he said. They walked the flower lined path hand in hand. Neither spoke a word only silence. He turned to face her and said, "we are home," Emma looked to see what he saw. There in front of her was the cute little cottage that she had so longed to find. He turned toward her and locked his gaze to hers. He moved in closer, their lips touch and Seth was gone.

Emma opened her eyes to a twig that had been snapped in two by a rabbit. It sat up on its hind legs while it stared at her and wiggled its nose. "It was just a dream, Mr. Bunny," she said as she watched him hop away.

Several weeks had passed and Emma lay awake at night. She had tried to solve the secret of who the artist might be of her lovely cottage. She realized that Seth once painted in this very room, but his name was Butter not Waters. Her feelings for him had grown as time passed on. For now she had to keep her feelings locked up inside of herself.

As the new librarian she thought of herself to be of some importance to the community when her name had been painted on the door in large gold letters. The books were few and mostly donated by the towns people. Emma had made her small room comfortable and cozy. She sewed curtains out of an old dress that was to small in size for her. She borrowed a table and two chairs from the back room of the Butter's mercantile. She made everything bright and cheery. "Just as a library should be," she thought to herself.

As she arranged some books she heard the door open. She turned to see Seth walk in; he was carrying a picnic basket.

"I brought lunch. Do you have time?" he asked as he bowed to her. He brought his other arm from behind his back to expose a bouquet of flowers.

"Beautiful flowers for a beautiful lady," he said.

Emma was tongue tied. She took the flowers from him and managed to say, "Thank you." As she walked to the counter to place them in a vase, she smelled them and smiled. She turned to face Seth as he snapped a black and red tablecloth.

It flowed perfectly over the table. He looked at her and smiled as she watched him lay things out by two's.

"I thought we would have an outdoors picnic indoors," Seth said as he smiled.

"We?" Emma asked with one eye raised.

"You are alone every day, I thought this would be fun," he replied.

"That's thoughtful of you, Seth," she said.

"I like to hear you call me by my name instead of butterball," he said.

"I can still call you that if you like," she said as they both giggled.

"I prefer Seth if you don't mind," he said.

"Well then, Seth, let's eat this yummy lunch you brought," Emma said as she sat on the small squeaky chair.

The first item Seth brought out of the basket was two mason jars filled with milk. He unscrewed the top of one and handed it to Emma.

"Thank you," she said as she took the jar from him.

"Your welcome," he replied.

Next were two plates he placed on the table in their proper position. All came out as twos. Two chicken legs, two biscuits, two portions of mashed potatoes with a small amount of gravy poured on top. He then reached into the basket and pulled out two forks and two cloth napkins that Mrs. Butter stitched the letter B on.

They ate their lunch as they made jokes and engaged in small talk. Emma had finally built up enough courage to ask Seth what she had so longed to hear the answer to.

"May I ask you something?" she asked.

"Yes you may," he said through a mouth full of food.

"Who is the Waters that painted that lovely cottage?" she boldly asked.

Quickly he answered, "Me."

Emma felt her heart leap into her throat as she asked, "You? How can it be you, your name is Butter?"

61

"That's a funny story. Would you like to hear it?" he asked. Emma nodded her head yes.

"When I decided to go to the university, Pop patted me on the back. Being the proud father and all. Well he said, 'Seth Butter, Attorney at Law.' It made me cringe when I heard that, so I took on my mother's maiden name. Pop ain't so happy about the whole thing, but he learned to accept it. So yes I'm Waters. Yes I'm the artist of the cottage and also the other paintings. Why do you ask?" Seth replied curiously.

"You?" she asked softly.

"Yes me, but you don't have to act like you're disappointed. Have you ever tried to live with the last name of Butter?" he replied.

"But how did you know?" she asked as she quickly ended her words.

"Know what?" he asked.

"The cottage, how did you know about the cottage?" she answered.

"I've been there. What exactly is your fascination with this place?" he asked

"Can you take me there?" Emma asked.

"It's at least a half day's ride through the woods, until you reach this ridge. It's a long way off route to any nearby town. But if you wish to see it, I can take you there," he said.

As Emma heard that the cottage actually existed, she was overly pleased that Seth would take her on this journey so she could view it with her own eyes.

"I would like nothing more than to go there with you," she replied happily.

"Then we go tomorrow," he said with exuberance.

"Tomorrow? Who will mind the library?" Emma asked.

"Do you see anyone knockin' the door down to get in here? Besides it will do us both good to get away for a while. We can saddle up and make a holiday of it. Don't you think that sounds nice?" he asked eagerly.

"Since you put it that way," Emma said as Seth interrupted and replied.

"We leave at first light," as he flashed her a hopeful smile.

Emma loved seeing him act so child-like happy and said, "Tomorrow morning it is."

Seth rubbed his hands together and said, "It will be a pleasant adventure, you just wait and see. Well, I have taken up enough of your busy day so I best be gettin' now."

Together they packed up the picnic basket and Emma said, "Thank you for thinking of me today. I had a rather enjoyable lunch."

"Your more than welcome, milady," Seth said as he took her hand into his and gently kissed it.

"Why, Seth Waters, you're quite charming when you want to be," Emma said as he picked up the basket and walked toward the door.

Seth turned and smiled and walked out the door. Before it had a chance to shut he poked his head back in and said, "I'll see you at dawn." Emma smiled and he closed the door.

After she closed the library Emma rushed home. She ate supper so quickly she thought she might be ill.

"Oh, dear, what is the hurry?" Mrs. Butter asked.

"I want to fill my tub and take a bath before Seth and I leave in the morning," Emma answered.

Mr. Butter looked at Seth with a peculiar eye and asked, "Oh? May I ask where you are going?"

"Just for a ride," Emma answered.

"Do you have riding britches, dear?" Mrs. Butter asked.

"No I don't. Do I need them where we are going ?" Emma asked as she looked at Seth.

He kept himself from choking on his food, but he managed to hoarsely answer, "It would probably be a good idea if you wore a pair."

"After supper we will go into the store and fetch what you will need for your outing tomorrow," Mrs. Butter said.

After the somewhat troubled conversation, supper was finished swiftly.

While Mrs. Butter and Emma search for the items needed Seth filled Emma's tub to make her evening more enjoyable. He kissed the rose he picked from his mother's bush and said, "I will never leave you, Emma Appleton." He laid the flower on the bed and left the room.

Emma awoke with a smile on her face and feeling exhilarated. The ray's of the sun peaked through her curtains. As she sat on the edge of the bed she stretched her arms to the air and said, "It's going to be a most heavenly day." She stood from her bed and picked up the rose that Seth left for her the night before. She smiled as she took in it's sweet fragrance and said, "I know." She picked the petals and tossed them into the water. She undressed and tested the temperature of the water with her toe. It was perfect. After her bath she quickly dressed and brushed her hair as she tied it into a ponytail and then into a braid that hung down her back. She dabbed on a few drops of lavender oil behind her ears and on her wrists. She gave herself one last look in the mirror, smiled and said, "You look silly." She walked out the door to meet her riding companion as it slammed behind her. She rushed down the stairs to find Seth waiting there with two horses.

"Are you ready for a ride in the country, milady?" he asked as he bowed to her while he held his hat in his hand and placed the other behind his back.

Emma smiled, curtsied and said, "Yes, milord."

Seth helped Emma mount her horse and said, "I have prepared a lunch for our pleasure when we see fit to be hungry, water for our pleasure when we see fit to wet our lips."

After he helped Emma, he jumped onto his own horse. The sound of their horses' hooves could be heard as they galloped out of town. The ride was long but Emma didn't mind, she was on an adventure with a handsome man. The birds flew about singing their songs, the sun was shining and a breeze pleasantly blew in her face.

"Seth, can we please stop so I can get a drink?" Emma asked.

"Yes, I think the horses might need some too," he said as he jumped from his horse. He pulled the canteen from his bag and handed it to her as she said, "Thank you. How much longer do we have to stay on this trail?"

She took a drink, wiped her mouth with her sleeve and handed the canteen back to him. He poured water into his cupped hand and let both horses drink from it. He then took a drink himself as he pointed to the path ahead. He wiped his mouth the same as Emma did and answered, "Do you see that ridge ahead? Over that is the path that leads to the cottage."

Emma's face lit up. "I'll race you," she said as she jumped on her horse, gave a swift snap to the reins and her horse began to run. Seth quickly returned the water bottle to the bag and did the same. When Emma reached the top she stopped her horse to stare at this perfection of nature as she said, "It's even more beautiful than I remember."

"What?" Seth asked with a confused look.

"Oh it's nothing," she answered as she waved her hand and smiled.

Emma followed Seth down the hill as he said, "Stay behind me, the path is narrow."

She inhaled the scent of wildflowers. She could hear the wind rustling the leaves about. A breeze blew her hair as it swirled the small curls that framed her face. The air seemed to be more pure and she tried to absorb as much of it as she possibly could.

"Seth, it's so beautiful, I wish that I could put it in a bottle and take it with me," Emma said.

The path was lined with all sorts of colors and types of flowers. The grass was long and lush as it swayed back and forth with the wind. It reminded her emeralds. Daisies popped up here and there through the meadow. A maple tree was to the side of the cottage, with long limbs and pretty burgundy leaves. The chimney was large and the roof was covered in moss. The large window in front had vines that grew around it's frame and up the side of the building.

"This place is absolutely breathtaking, Seth, I never want to leave here," Emma said cheerfully.

They went past the cottage right to the big tree and climbed down from their horses.

"This is a nice place to relax," Seth said.

"Does anyone live here?" Emma asked.

"I've been here several times and never saw a soul," Seth answered.

He pulled a blanket from his bag and laid it under the tree and they started to unpack the stuff he had packed. As they made their selves comfortable on the blanket Seth quickly sprang to his feet and said, "I almost forgot." He reached deep into his bag and pulled out a bottle of wine and two objects wrapped in the same cloth napkins she had saw the day before.

"What's that?" she asked.

"I've been saving this for quite sometime. For a special occasion," he answered.

He sat down once again and unwrapped the glasses and uncorked the wine. They ate their sandwiches, drank wine and exchanged conversation. Emma dripped wine down her chin and giggled. Seth reached over to wipe it from her face and their eyes locked onto one another. Seth took advantage of the moment and leaned in to kiss her. As their lips touched, Emma's heart began to race. Seth immediately went into retreat and said, "I should not have allowed that to happen. I apologize." He then hung his head down.

"I'm happy that it did," Emma replied.

He raised his head and looked at her confusingly as he said, "I was under the impression that you wanted a gentleman."'

"You apologized didn't you?" Emma replied with a smile.

"May I?" he asked as he moved closer to her. Emma nodded her head once. He closed his eyes and softly kissed her forehead. Emma felt as if her heart leapt from her body. He gently touched her face with his hand and kissed her lips and her cheek. He looked up at her as he moved her hair and kissed her neck. Emma felt a tingling surge move through out her body that produced excitement and the need for wanting more. Her chest began to heave and Seth noticed her nipples protruded through her blouse. He brushed his hand across them and Emma deeply inhaled. He began to unbutton her blouse. Emma tried to talk but he put his finger over her lips and said, "Shhh."

He slid her blouse off one shoulder and kissed it as he did the other the same. As Emma's bare breasts were exposed Seth cupped one in his hand and gave her nipple a flick of his tongue. Emma tilted her head back and shook with excitement. He did the other, Emma moaned. Seth could feel himself needing her. As he leaned back to make a space for them Emma could see his bulging manhood. Her body ached for more of his touch. The sensations were unclear to her but she knew she wanted him.

Seth laid her down gently and kissed her lips as he moved downward.

He thought how soft her skin was and how she smelled of lavender. She was not a girl but a woman.

He slid his hand down to her patch and gave a little squeeze and Emma yelped loudly. Seth so enjoyed her noise and quickly began to undress her. He kissed her belly as she squirmed with delight. He then began to undress himself. Emma helped as she kissed his neck softly. She ran her fingers up and down his back feeling every ripple and muscle. His body was firm and she could feel the strength he so possessed. She memorized every part of him.

As she lay on her back, Seth gazed at her exposed, naked

body that lay before him. He kissed her thigh as he touched her fur once again and felt the wetness she had for him. She tilted her head back and moaned in excitement. He moved his body atop of hers. She felt his hardness press against her legs. She was eager to feel him inside of her.

Their eyes met and they were fascinated by one another for a moment. Emma closed her eyes as Seth moaned with pleasure as he slid himself inside her warm opening. Emma held her breath for a brief moment, then exhaled as she felt him enter her untouched area of sensation.

He began to slide in and out of her, slow at first as not to hurt her. With her eyes closed and her head tilted back she enjoyed what she felt.

Seth thrust himself deeper into her cavity and began to move more rapidly. Emma grasped the blanket in her palms as she made fists. She created noises she never believed possible.

Seth took one side of her bottom into his hand as he pushed his manhood even deeper inside of her.

Emma moved her body with his as she grappled his back and held him tightly. The two dripped with the sweat of desire as their bodies connected and they became one. The heat rose as his thrusts became more dominating. A breathless rush of burning passion rose in their bodies as they reached the tip of a perfect orgasm. With one more vigorous thrust they erupted with the perfect climax of ecstasy as they cried out in pleasure. The cry was so loud the birds in the trees were frightened and flew away.

Seth lay atop of Emma, consumed with soaking in all they could within one another.

Seth moved the hair from her face and looked into her eyes as he replied softly, "I love you, Emma Appleton, will you do me the honor of becoming my wife?"

Emma was overwhelmed with emotion and her body flowed with fascinating sensations. She smiled at him and answered, "Yes! Yes! Yes! I will be your wife."

Seth was overjoyed with her response and relished her in kisses and I love yous.

They lay under the tree as they kissed and caressed each other for what seemed to be hours. They engaged in lovemaking once more; it burned with more desire and lust than the first.

As Emma pulled on her boots Seth asked, "Remember when I brought you the lavender package?"

"Yes," Emma answered.

"Why did your hand have that odd glow and why were you holding it over my ma?" Seth asked softly as he continued to dress himself.

"Can we leave now?" Emma snapped.

Seth became confused at her sudden change in mood and asked, "What? What did I say?"

"Never mind," Emma replied.

With nothing more said Emma had time to soothe herself and said, "I'm sorry for being so short with you. Can we talk of this at another time? I would just like to get home."

"We can go if that's what you wish," he said as he walked to her, cupped her face in his hands and gently kissed her.

They finished packing up their belongings and began their ride up the hill. The ride was silent for some time. They stopped for water but not a word was spoken. Seth remained calm but was beginning to become frustrated with the silence.

"Emma I know that you are angry with me but I'm hopeful that this doesn't change what we feel for one another," Seth said.

"I had the most amazing day of my life. I received a marriage proposal but because I am displeased in some way doesn't change my love for you. I still want to be your wife. To relieve any misunderstandings I still love you," she said with a smile.

"Okay, my darling, I was just hoping that I wouldn't have

to take you back under the tree and you know," he said. After a short pause he laughed.

Emma blushed and giggled.

As they reached the end of their path, Emma stopped her horse and looked at Seth as she said, "I'm not quite ready to share our news just yet. Could we keep it between us for a while?"

"If that makes you happy but I must admit that I can't wait long. I want to make you my wife quickly as I can," he replied as he leaned toward her to kiss her.

"Thank you," she said with a smile as their lips parted.

"I love you, Emma," he said lovingly as he looked into her eyes

"I love you too," she returned.

They continued their ride into town as they laughed and carried on as if they were children once more.

Chapter Seven

It was dusk when they rode into town. Mrs. Butter ran out as they approached the mercantile and shouted, "Your mother has taken ill and you are needed at home right away," she said anxiously.

Emma became frantic as the tears began to roll down her cheeks. She turned to face Seth as he said, "You ain't alone. I'll ride with you."

Emma managed a small smile as she said, "Thank you."

Emma rode so quickly Seth remained some time behind her. When she had reached her destination she jumped from her horse as swiftly as she rode and ran into the house. Seth jumped from his horse and grabbed the reins to walk the horses into the barn for fresh water and food.

Toby met Emma at the door as she came slamming through, he jumped up and wrapped his legs around her and said, "Sister, you're back."

Emma squeezed him tightly, "Sister, I can't breathe," he managed to say while he tried to catch his breath.

"Oh I'm sorry, little brother, I'm just happy to see you," she said with a smile as she loosened her grip. She kissed him on the forehead, ruffled his hair and set him down.

"I don't like kisses, only hugs—yuck," he said as he vigorously wiped his forehead with his sleeve.

Emma bent down and turned him in a circle as she said, "Let me look at you. You are quite the little man ain't you?"

"I a boy," Toby replied sternly as he placed his hands on his hips.

Emma giggled and said, "Yes you are," as she stood and faced her father and asked, "Is Mama in her room?"

"She's real sick," he said as he lowered his head.

"I know, Papa, that's why I'm here," she replied. Emma turned when she heard the door open to see Seth walk in.

"Toby, this is my friend Seth, Seth, this is my baby brother Toby." Emma said.

Seth offered his hand and said, "I'm pleased to meet you, young man."

Once again Toby placed his hands on his hips and said, "I not a man, I a boy." He then sighed loudly.

"Pardon me boy, I didn't know," Seth said as he and Emma giggled to themselves.

"Sir, I'm pleased to meet you," Seth said as he offered his hand to Thomas.

"Likewise," Thomas returned.

Emma could see in her father's face that he was distraught. She squatted down to Toby and said, "I'm going to see Mama now, you stay here with my friend, he is a very nice man. You best mind him ya hear?"

"Yes, sister, I will," he said as he slipped his hand into Seth's.

"Don't worry about us, you go be with your mother she's waiting for you. I'll be waiting for you when you return," Seth said.

Emma whispered, "I love you," as she turned and walked away.

Emma peaked around the bedroom door just as her father snuck up behind her. He flung the door open and barged in to the room as he said, "Olyvia, Emma is here."

"Is she awake?" Emma asked.

"Yes," Thomas answered as he laid his wife's hand on his own.

"Hi, Mama, I'm here," Emma said softly as she slowly crept up to her bedside.

"Here, Emma, you can sit in my chair. I'll let the two of you visit," Thomas said as he stood.

Emma was thrown back by the mood change in her father from when he stood in the kitchen some time earlier.

Thomas kissed Olyvia on the forehead and said, "I love you." He rubbed Emma's back and said, "It's nice to see you again." Emma only smiled back at him as she quietly sat in the chair and waited or a response from her mother. She was oblivious to her illness. Not knowing how well or how ill she really was.

"Come closer, my love, I want to see your face," her mother said as she motioned her hand.

Emma stood from her chair and sat on the bed next to her mother. Olyvia patted her hand and said, "You look pretty."

"You look pretty too, Mama," Emma said as she cleared her throat and smiled.

"You are to kind," Olyvia replied as she scooted herself up into a sitting position.

"Mama, are you going to die?" Emma asked as she held back from her tearful emotion.

"Yes, but not today," she answered.

Emma lost control and laid her head on her mother's legs as she began to weep.

"Don't worry my love it will all work itself out," Olyvia said as she ran her fingers over Emma's hair.

Emma lifted her head and looked at her mother through tear filled eyes as she said, "But, Mama, I don't want you to die."

"Let's talk about you. How have you been?" Olyvia asked as she smiled.

Emma wiped her tears that rolled down her cheeks and answered, "I'm a librarian now."

"Yes I have heard, and I am very proud of you," her mother replied.

"I have a room over the Butter's store and I have my very own bathtub," Emma said.

"How on earth did you manage to get your own bathtub?" Olyvia asked.

Emma took a deep breath and answered, "Seth Butter, but he changed his name because he is studying at the university to be a lawyer and he said have you tried to be a lawyer with the last name Butter?" Emma let out a little giggle and continued on, "He bought me a tub and lavender oil just like yours, Mama, I thought he was an ass oh sorry, Mama, we went for a ride today so we could get away for a while it was nice that's why I am wearing these riding britches that Mrs. Butter gave me." Emma took a long deep breath, sighed and smiled at her mother as she sat back in her chair.

"You said a lot without even taking a breath. Are you sure that's everything?" her mother asked with a little giggle and a smile.

Emma sat up and said, "I'll tell you again, Mama, if you want me to."

"I heard plenty, thank you," she said.

"Mama, do you want me to take your illness away?" Emma asked.

"Your so sweet to think of me but I don't think I will ever be well again," her mother replied.

"Can I try?" Emma asked.

"You're a persistent little thing ain't ya?" she said as she coughed.

"Look at you, Mama, at how sick you have become, can I please try?" Emma asked.

"Only once," she answered.

"Okay, Mama, only once I promise," Emma said.

She sat on the side of the bed, placed her hand atop of Olyvia's abdomen and closed her eyes paused for a moment to concentrate. She began as she said softly, "I wish you well, I wish you well, I wish you well." At that moment Emma's palm began to glow with the beautiful blue light.

Olyvia was astonished with the gift her daughter possessed within the palm of her hand. She shifted her body to see more clearly and the beautiful glow ended as quickly as it came about.

"How do you feel, Mama," Emma asked as she removed her hand and smiled at her mother.

"If you help me up I can meet your Seth," Olyvia said as she swung her legs around to the side of the bed.

"Are you sure that you are feeling well enough to get out of bed?" Emma asked.

"Yes I am," she answered.

Emma stood at her mother's side and helped her slide on her robe. She took her arm into her own and they walked slowly to the door as Olyvia firmly gripped Emma's hand to keep her balance.

As the two women enter the kitchen Thomas stood and then Seth, he stared in amazement. Thomas was not in disbelief, he only smiled at his wife for he knew what his daughter had accomplished.

Toby ran to his mother and wrapped his arms around her legs as he excitedly said, "Mama, Mama, you're better." He released his embrace to place his arm on the back of her legs as she walked and said, "I help to."

Thomas pulled out a chair and helped her to sit down as Toby adjusted the skirt of her nightdress and robe and said, "There, Mama, you look pretty."

After Olyvia positioned herself she tilted her head back, smiled and said, "I would just love a cup of coffee, my dear."

"Would you like anything else," he asked attentively.

"Just coffee, thank you," she answered as she held out her hand to Seth and asked, "Is this your friend you have spoken so highly of?"

Seth stood and politely kissed the top of her hand and said, "Glad to make your acquaintance, Mrs. Appleton."

"Oh sit down, there is no need for you to be so formal," she said as she motioned her hand to him.

"Seth is studying to become a hot shot lawyer," Thomas said jokingly.

" Ain't that nice, I bet your folks are proud. I don't mean to pry but why ain't we heard of you til' now? Don't your folks own the mercantile?" Olyvia asked.

"That's a good question." Emma said as she looked at Seth curiously.

"My parents had me late in life. They told me that I was too ill to play with the other children. They were and still are good parents but I think that they were just embarrassed by their age and were trying to protect me. Miss Rose visited in the evenings three nights a week. She taught me the same lessons as the other children. When I was ready I left for the university and found that I ain't ill at all and all is well, wouldn't you say?" he said as he raised his arms in the air.

Everyone was amused, but not Emma, she became angry and said, "You never told me that story."

"I never thought it being of importance," Seth replied calmly.

"Seth is a good boy; why don't you give him a chance— geez," her father replied as he patted Seth on the back.

Emma was astonished by the comment her father had just made. "No one will ever be good enough for MY daughter," he always said.

"So tell me, son, what brings you home now?" Thomas asked as he sat in a chair next to his wife.

"Well sir, I'm home on holiday for the summer season.

Thought I might help out the folks with the store and all. In the fall I go back to study," Seth answered.

Emma sat in frustrated silence and she glared at the two men while they conversed.

"Well, my lovely wife, have you had enough excitement for one day? Would you like for me to walk you back to bed?" Thomas asked.

"I am so drowsy, I would love for you to walk with me. Seth, it was nice to meet you," she said as she smiled and stood.

"And you, ma'am," he replied as he also stood.

"Thank you for bringing her to me," Olyvia said as she kissed Emma's forehead and smiled at her.

"Oh yes, ma'am, Emma is a very stubborn woman and nothing would have kept her away from here," he said as he looked at Emma and smiled.

"That she is," Olyvia replied with an understanding grin as she blew Toby a kiss.

Emma looked up at her and said, "Good night, Mama."

Toby wrapped himself around his mother's legs just as he had done earlier and said, "Good night, Mama."

"You never told me of those things before," Emma retorted.

"Can we talk of this later?" he asked as he motioned his head toward Toby. Emma turned to look at him, he sat with his arms crossed on the table as he grinned from ear to ear.

A few moments later Thomas returned and said, "Your mother would like to speak with you, Emma."

She sat on the edge of the bed next to her mother as Olyvia said, "Your Seth is a nice young man. You should hold on to that one."

Emma smiled and replied, "Yes, Mama. Would you like for me to stay on for a while?" As she reached for her mother's hand.

"I think it would be best, only until I'm able to move around by myself," her mother answered.

"Okay, Mama, but for now you need rest," Emma said as she stood and kissed her mother on the forehead.

As Emma opened the door her mother said, "Thank you for being my daughter."

"I'll see you in the morning, Mama," she said and shut the door quietly behind her.

The two men sat at the table chatting away. Emma sat down with them and said, "Mama has asked me to stay on until she's able to do chores and things."

"You can stay as long as you like," Thomas said as he and Toby grinned from ear to ear just as Toby had done earlier.

Seth sat quietly and listened to Emma's announcement. He stood suddenly and said, "I should be gettin' back now, it's been a long day. It was nice to meet you, sir."

"Likewise, I hope we can meet again real soon." Thomas replied as they shook hands.

"Until next time then," Seth said with a smile.

Emma stood and said, "I'll walk you out."

Seth looked at Toby and said in a deep voice, "Nice to meet you, boy."

Toby cleared his throat and as he tried to mock Seth he said, "You too, sir." He stood with an odd expression on his face as he struggled to get it back to normal everyone laughed at him.

When Seth heard the door latch closed he swiftly reached for Emma's hand, he held it in his own with a loose grip as they walked to the barn.

"How much time do you think your mother will need?" he asked.

"I don't rightly know," Emma answered.

"I will miss you," he said as he walked the horses from the barn.

Emma smiled and replied, "I will miss you too."

Seth cupped her face in his hands and looked deep into her eyes and said, "I had the most wonderful day. Soon I will have you as my wife." He gently kissed her lips and said, "I love you."

"I love you too," she replied.

The moon was full and shined enough light that she could see his face as he climbed upon his horse. The leather of the saddle crunched as he leaned down to capture one more token of affection as he said, "I'm not too far away if you need me."

"I know, my darling," she replied.

As he sat up the saddle crunched once more and echoed in the silence of the night. He looked down at her as she blew him a kiss. He smiled and rode away. Emma stood quietly while the moon's light surrounded her. She listened to the sound of his horse as it trotted and she could hear it no more.

"Mmm, what is that smell?" Olyvia said as she entered the kitchen.

"Well good morning, Mother, our daughter made us breakfast. Sit and eat with us," Thomas said as he pulled out a chair for her.

"How are you feeling this morning, Mama?" Emma asked as she placed a plate on the table for her mother.

"I feel a little weak, but I know that once I eat this breakfast I will feel much better," she answered.

"The wash is hangin' out to dry, Toby is fed and outdoors playing. I told him I would come out with him if you didn't need me right away," Emma said.

"I can manage. Go ahead be with your brother; he has missed you," her mother answered as she put a bite of food in her mouth.

"I won't be far so if you need me, holler real loud." She kissed her mother and left to join Toby outdoors.

"She's grown to be a strong woman. And beautiful, like her mother," Thomas replied.

"Flattery will get you everywhere, Thomas Appleton," she said in a playful voice.

He put his arm around her shoulder and gave her a little squeeze. Olyvia blushed and said, "Oh Thomas."

"I'm pleased that Emma is back home. But what concerns me is, for how long," Thomas said.

"Let's not rush our time with her," Olyvia said as she took a sip of her coffee.

"What about this boy of hers?" Thomas asked.

"She ain't spoke much of him but seems like a nice enough young man and we know he comes from good stock," she answered.

"Well I ain't gonna make it easy for him," Thomas replied with a smile.

"We wouldn't have it any other way," Olyvia said with a little giggle.

"I best be gittin' to the field," Thomas said as he stood and gulped down his remaining coffee.

"You go. I'll be fine," she said.

"I won't be far so if you need me, holler real loud," he said mockingly.

Olyvia gave him a little wave of her hand and said, "Will you just leave?"

Thomas sat back in his chair and pulled her onto his lap. He wrapped his arms around her and said softly, "I love you, Olyvia."

"Mr. Appleton what if someone were to find us like this," she replied jokingly.

Thomas laughed, he lifted her back to her chair and kissed her on the cheek as he said, "I'll be back shortly."

The door shut and Olyvia sat back in her chair with a smile and sighed as she took another sip of her coffee.

Emma knew where she would find Toby. She paid close attention to the nature that surrounded her as she walked slowly to their secret place. As she walked nearer she could see that he had been waiting for her.

"Sister, look," he said as he held up a book. She knew it. She had read it to him so many times before.

This put a smile upon her face as she sat next to him she made herself comfortable and said, "I remember that book," she thought of how it had brought her imagination to life.

"Will you read to me please, sister," Toby pleaded. As she opened the book he asked, "Will we ever go there?"

"Where?" she asked confused.

"There," he said as he pointed to the picture in the book.

"Oh yes we will drink from glass cups and eat expensive food from real china plates," she answered as her mind wandered to a place no one else could travel to.

"Sister, sister?" Toby quietly shouted.

"Yes, little brother," she answered.

"Can we go see Mama?" he asked.

"That is a good idea," she replied.

They stood and brushed themselves off and began the walk back to the house.

Toby slipped his little hand into hers and said, "I miss you when you ain't here, sister."

"I miss you too," she said.

"Good," he replied sternly.

"You are quite the young man, I mean young boy," she said with a smile.

"That's okay," he said.

"What?" she asked.

"You call me man. I play games with Seth," he answered.

Emma laughed. They played and exchanged jokes as they walked. Emma's heart leapt with joy as she watched Toby so peaceful and happy. Winter would be approaching soon and he had already began to cough. She had hoped his life would be filled with happiness and he would take it with him as he grew into a man.

Chapter Eight

After Emma had cooked supper, she served her father and Toby. She tiptoed into her mother's room to observe if she was resting comfortably. As she turned to leave the room Olyvia opened her eyes and said, "Thank you, Emma, for all you do."

Emma walked to the bed and pulled the covers up farther as she said, "I know you do, Mama, now please try to get some rest." She kissed her on the cheek and left the room.

Thomas finished his meal and went to his favorite chair as usual. When he lit his pipe Emma could smell the tobacco in the kitchen where she stood. When she had finished cleaning up she joined Toby and her father in the other room. She sat on the floor with the view of her father before her and asked, "Papa, will you play a song for me?"

Thomas picked up his violin as the pipe hung from his lips. He played a slow and simple song. When he had completed his serenade he smiled at Emma and said, "That one was for my little girl."

"Thank you, Papa, that was real pretty," she replied as she returned the smile.

Thomas sat his violin back in it's rightful place and stirred the coals of the fire as he said, "I'm sorry."

"Toby, I think it's time for bed," Emma said softly.

"Why, sister? I not tired, why do I have to go to bed if I ain't tired?" Toby whined.

"Because this is the time of night that little brothers go to bed," Emma replied.

"But," Toby tried to plead as his father stopped him and said, "You mind your sister now and do what she says."

"Yes, papa," he said as he whined, hung his head low and drug his feet while he walked to Emma. He kissed her and slowly said the words, "Good night sister." As he tried to arouse some kind of sympathy from her.

"Good night Toby, I'll see you in the morning," she said as she tried to conceal her smile from him.

Toby bid his father a good night in the same fashion as he did his sister. Thomas also hid his amusement.

With his head hung low Toby scuffed his feet as he walked away.

With Toby out of the room Emma said, "I'm sorry too, Papa," as she moved herself closer to his chair.

"I can't lose you and your mother too. I wouldn't know what to do with myself," he replied.

Emma laid her head on his knee and said, "Papa, you ain't lost me and Mama ain't goin' nowhere for a very long time."

"You only fixed the outside and only for a short time. She truly is ill," he replied.

Emma's eyes widened in surprise as she lifted her head and looked at her father. She asked, "You know?"

"I've known since your gift has awakened. Don't worry. I ain't gonna tell a soul," he said with a comforting smile.

"Thank you, Papa," she said.

"It's getting late, I think I'll head to bed myself," he said.

"Okay, Papa," Emma said as she looked up at him.

"Don't worry, little girl, your secret is safe with me," he said as he bent down to kiss her on the forehead. He smiled, stood from his chair as he towered over her and then walked away.

It had been several weeks since Emma's arrival.

"Mmm, that smells yummy," Emma thought as she swiftly jumped from her large bed and ran for the kitchen to find her mother as she cooked breakfast.

"Good morning, how did you sleep?" Olyvia asked her.

"Mama, what are you doing?" Emma shouted at her.

"Emma, there is no need to be so agitated," she replied.

"I'm sorry, Mama, but shouldn't you be resting?" Emma said calmly.

"I feel fine and I'm trying very hard to have a nice day. So why don't you get yourself dressed and eat your breakfast before it gets cold," she replied.

Without another word spoken, Emma turned and did exactly what her mother had said. She got dressed and pulled her hair back into a ponytail, pinched her cheeks for color and rushed back to the kitchen.

As she sat at the table her mother sat a plate of food in front of her and announced, "Why don't you invite your Seth over for supper some night?"

Emma had a blank look upon her face and asked, "I should?"

"He seems like a nice boy and I think your papa has taken a fancy to him," she answered.

"He has?" Emma asked with surprise.

"Why don't you take a break from chores today and go into town. While you are there why don't you ask Seth out for supper tonight?" she replied.

"Tonight?" Emma asked in a high pitched tone of voice.

"Yes tonight. I want you to march your pretty little self into town and ask him," she replied.

""Yes, Mama," Emma said. She knew that there would be no argument won with her mother.

"That's a good girl, you best get a move on you have a big day ahead of you," Olyvia said happily.

"Seth slept in Emma's room while she was away. As he opened his eyes he saw the cottage painting and smiled. He thought of Emma and realized he had missed her terribly. He rolled toward the other side of the bed and ran his hand over her pillow, he could still smell her scent of lavender on it. He felt himself begin to get hard as he imagined her naked body lying there next to his.

Seth walked in the door and immediately saw her as she sat in the kitchen. Her long hair tied in a silk ribbon, he loved the way the curls spun down her back. He suddenly became flustered. He stood for a moment to collect himself and walked into the kitchen with a smile.

She turned to look at him as he flashed her a half grin and said, "Good morning, girl."

"Seth, you stop that right now. This young lady is here to give you an important invitation," Mrs. Butter said as she playfully slapped his arm.

"Oh does she?" he asked as he lifted one eyebrow at her.

"Yes, Mama asked me to invite you to supper tonight," Emma replied.

"Well, I best accept," Seth said with a smile.

"Is five o'clock okay?" she asked.

"That is a perfect time," he answered.

"Well I best be goin', I want to make sure everything is in order at the library," Emma said as she stood.

Seth helped her with her chair and asked, "If you don't mind the company, I'll walk with you."

"I don't mind at all. Thank you, Mrs. Butter, for the tea, it was a pleasure to sit and visit with you," Emma replied with a happy smile.

"I enjoyed it too. You come visit me again real soon, dear," Mrs. Butter said.

Seth and Emma turned to leave as Mrs. Butter shouted, "What about your breakfast, son?"

Without a break of his gaze toward Emma or his smile he

slightly turned his head and replied through his teeth, "Ma, I'll eat later."

"Young'uns," Mrs. Butter said to herself as she shook her head.

Seth and Emma strolled the wooden sidewalk he asked, "Is your mother well?"

"She made breakfast this morning and did chores," Emma answered.

"I reckon that's a good sign ain't it?" he replied.

"I'm afraid she may be doin' too much," Emma said.

They approached the door of the library, Emma reached into her pouch to retrieve the key. Once inside Seth swiftly wrapped his arms around her waist and pulled her body close to his own and said, "I have missed you terribly."

Emma smiled and wrapped her arms around his neck as they shared a passionate kiss.

"Everything seems to be in order here," Emma said as she giggled.

"Well, Miss Appleton, I'm surprised at you. This was all just a little game to lure me here," he said as he looked into her eyes and giggled himself.

Emma laid her head on his chest and said, "You found me out and I'm so ashamed."

"I'm happy that you did, you little vixen, you," he replied.

"You best be kind to your soon-to-be wife," Emma said.

"Oh yes, ma'am!" Seth said with stern sarcasm.

"I best be gettin' back home I've gone too lengthy a time already," Emma said.

Seth broke the connection between them and asked, "I thought your home was with me?"

"Yes, darling, it is. I have to make sure my mama is well before I leave her to fend for herself," Emma replied sadly.

"How long will that take?" he asked.

"I don't rightly know," she answered.

"We both know what you can do for her, so why haven't you?" he said.

"We both know what?" she asked.

"My ma has or should I say had an illness that caused shortness of breath. Sometimes it made it difficult for her to function. Now she does things that she hasn't been able to do in ages, ever since that day in your room," Seth answered confidently and tilted his head to one side as he waited for an explanation.

"Really?" Emma asked excitedly as she turned away from him, not to reveal her smile.

"Look at me, woman! I don't rightly care what you are or are not capable of doing. I just want to get married and someday have babies," he exclaimed as he grabbed her shoulders and swung her around to face him.

By this point Emma's eyes had filled with tears. Seth moved the hair from her face as he said gently, "I love you, do you understand that?"

"Tonight after supper I will tell you when I can come home. Will that please you?" she replied in a displeasing tone while she cleared her throat.

"There is no need to be unpleasant. I am only eager to make you my wife. To answer your question, yes that outright pleases me," he replied.

"I want the same thing," she whispered as she buried her head in his chest and began to sob.

"I can only hope that it all sways in our direction," he said as he runs his hands up and down her back.

"Me too," she said through her sobbing.

"Seth placed his hands on her shoulders to look at her, he moved the hair from her face once again and wiped the tears from her cheeks. Gently he raised her face as he placed his fingers under her chin and said, "Look at me, pretty lady. Do you know how badly I yearn to feel your body next to mine at night? Your beautiful face is the last thing I want to see before I close my eyes at night and the radiant sparkle in your eyes when I rise in the morning. I want our life to have meaning. I want for our love to be so strong for one another that it leaves no room for anything else. Are you hearing what I am saying to you? I love you. I love you so much I can't think of anything else. So won't you please help your mother's recovery along and come back to me."

Tears rolled down Emma's face as she stared into his eyes. She stood in silence with only one thought in her head, to rush out the door and marry him. At that point she knew it couldn't happen.

"Don't cry," he said as he handed her his handkerchief. She wiped her face and nose and proceeded to hand it back to him.

He smiled and said, "That's okay you hold on to it for me. Don't you think it best to head back home now? Your family is probably worried of your whereabouts."

"Seth," she began to say as he put his finger against her lips and said, "I know," as he took her hands into his own and said, "I love you."

"I love you too," she replied.

"I would like to walk you to the path, if I could," he said with a smile.

"I would like that very much," she said as she returned the gesture.

They walked hand in hand to the door and shared one more tender kiss.

We should not let anything get in the way of our love and being together," Seth said.

"Soon I promise," Emma replied with a smile.

They slowly walked along the dirt street, a dusty wind blew around them as the sound of horses hooves and carriages pass them by.

Emma held the handkerchief over her face and asked, "You haven't mentioned a word of your studies. When do you leave to go back to the university?"

"I leave in about four weeks and I'll be back in time for

Christmas. I'll stay on through to the new year," he answered.

"That's quite some time to be away from home," she replied through the handkerchief.

Seth looked at her through one eye and said, "Only several months."

They stopped at the opening of the path that ran aside the river which led to her house. It was not easily visible with the tall tree's that grew along the other side of the path.

Emma stuffed the handkerchief into her skirt pocket as she looked at Seth and said, "This is where we part, at least until tonight."

"I wish you knew how badly I want to take you into my arms," Seth said with fire in his voice as he shook his fists playfully.

"Soon enough," Emma said as she stood and stared at him and his childishness that caused her to giggle.

"Okay," he said as he hung his head low. He quickly lifted his head to look at her and with plenty of excitement he said, "I'll see you in a few short hours."

"Okay, Seth I'll see you then, I love you," she said with a smile as she turned to walk away.

"I love you too," he returned.

"Bye," she said with a little feminine wave to him.

"Bye," he said as he waved back to her.

Seth watched her body sway from side to side as she walked down the path. He stood in silence as if he were in a spell and said to himself, "Oh yes, I will make that woman mine."

At four, Emma, in her cluttered state of mind, frantically ran around her house as she prepared for Seth's arrival.

"Why don't you relax a bit," her mother asked as she stood and smiled and admired her daughter's enthusiasm.

"I just want it to be perfect for him, Mama," Emma answered while she tried to catch her breath.

"It will all work itself out, my love," her mother replied.

"I guess your right, Mama. He's eatin' supper and if it's bad it will be your fault because you cooked it," Emma said jokingly.

"You are quite the little jokester ain't you," her mother said as she playfully waved her hand at Emma.

Seth arrived on time with a bouquet of flowers for Olyvia.

"Thank you Seth their beautiful. I'll get a vase and we can admire them while we eat," she said as she walked away.

"You're welcome, Mrs. Appleton," he replied.

Emma stood patiently and waited for her gift.

"This is for you, Emma," Seth said.

"What is this?" she asked with a disappointed look upon her face as she glared at the object she held in the palm of her hand.

"It's from a special place we visited not to long ago," he answered.

Emma blushed and did not speak another word as she quickly tucked the pretty pink rock into her skirt pocket.

"Come in, my boy, and have a seat," Thomas said as he patted Seth on the back with one hand and shook with the other.

When the meal was finished Thomas stood and said, "That was good, Mother," he kissed her on the cheek and assumed the evening position on his chair. He lit his pipe and as it hung from his mouth he built a fire and said, "Come sit, Seth, and relax a little."

The two women remained in the kitchen to clean up and carry on a conversation of their own. They paid no mind to the men and their discussion.

"Come in, have a seat," Thomas said as he motioned to the sofa.

"Thank you, sir," Seth replied as he sat down.

"So tell me what are your intentions with my daughter?" Thomas asked as he took a deep breath from his pipe and sat back in his chair.

"I care very much for Emma, my intentions are purely honorable," Seth answered as he looked toward her. She hadn't a notion of what they were discussing. She only smiled and continued with her task at hand.

"That's one in your favor. Because if my daughter sheds one tear caused by you, then you will answer to me," Thomas said as he leaned forward in his chair and asked, "Is that understood?"

Seth had become frightened and Thomas could hear it in his voice as he replied, "Oh no, sir, I would never."

"You best not," Thomas rudely interrupted.

"Yes sir," Seth replied politely.

"You seem like a nice boy," Thomas said as he leaned forward in his chair and motioned for Seth to come closer, "It would be a shame if I had to take care of you. If you get my meaning," he said as he sat back in his chair with a smile and took another puff from his pipe while he gave Seth a little wink.

"I, sir, would also feel the same if Emma were my daughter," Seth replied quickly.

"I like your attitude, son," Thomas said as he drew in more from his pipe and gave a little smile from the corner of his mouth.

Toby sat at the table to eat his pie. The sticky syrup from the apples smeared over his face. Olyvia smiled at him as she walked by with a serving tray of coffee and pie. She and Emma served the men and took their places next to them.

"So tell me, Seth, how are your studies coming along?" Olyvia asked as she took a sip of her coffee.

Seth quickly swallowed his pie without chewing and answered, "Well, ma'am, it's surely hard work but I have received a large amount of knowledge."

"We sure wouldn't want an ignorant lawyer would we?" Thomas sarcastically blurted out.

"No, sir! We surely wouldn't want that," Seth quickly retorted.

91

Thomas was surprised by Seth's quick response. He concealed his smile and continued to smoke his pipe quietly.

"It's time for bed, Toby. Wash your hands and face please," Olyvia said.

"But, Mama, I don't want to go to bed. I want to stay up and listen," he whined.

"Listen to your mama, boy," Thomas said in a stern voice.

"Geez," Toby said.

Toby lowered his head and began his evening ritual, he said all of his good nights. He left the room in his usual manner with his head bowed and scuffed his feet as he tried to play on everyone's sympathy. The family kept their mouths covered to hide their amusement of his comical drama.

The adults continued to visit with one another, for what seemed to be hours. They laughed and enjoyed each other's company.

"I best be getting back," Seth said as he sat his cup down.

"So soon?" Emma asked.

"Pop has an early delivery in the morning and I would like to help him unload," Seth said as he stood.

Thomas stood and they shook hands as Seth said, "Sir," while Thomas patted him on the back.

"Nice seeing you again," Thomas said.

"Ma'am, it's been a pleasure, thank you for the meal," Seth replied as he politely kissed the top of her hand.

"Please come again," Olyvia said.

"Thank you, I will surely do that," Seth said with a smile as he bowed his head to her.

"Mama, I'm gonna walk Seth out I will be right back in," Emma said as she stood.

"You ain't coming home are you?" Seth asked as they walked with their arms interwoven within one another.

"Well," she said.

"Well what?" he asked.

She turned away from him and answered in a sad voice, "Tomorrow, I'm coming home tomorrow."

Seth quickly turned her around to reveal her smile and said, "You have made this man very happy. We will celebrate with something special," as he pulled her close to him.

"Seth, what if Papa finds us like this?" Emma replied playfully.

He grabbed her behind and pulled her closer to his body as he asked, "And what about like this?"

Emma giggled and said, "I really need to get back inside."

He kissed her cheek and said, "Until tomorrow, my darling," as he bowed.

He jumped on his horse in a most dashing way. He fumbled and instead of an inquired seat on the saddle he landed on the horn. Never to lose his composure, he smiled and tried to situate himself. He sat tall, cleared his throat and said, "Tomorrow, my dear."

Emma stood in silence as she watched him try to hide his discomfort.

"Until tomorrow," she said as she curtsied.

Being careful not to move to much he blew her a kiss.

She returned the notion and he rode away.

As she walked back to the house she could hear, "Ow, ow, ow." She only smiled.

Emma sat on the sofa and Thomas said, "I best be gettin' to bed; tomorrow comes early." He kissed his wife.

"Good night, princess," he said to Emma as he patted her on the head.

Emma smiled and said, "Good night, Papa."

"That was some meal mother," he said while he rubbed his round belly, as he walked away.

"It was a nice evening," Olyvia said.

"I thought so," Emma replied as she sat in her father's chair next to her mother's.

"Mama, are you feeling well these days?" Emma asked.

"Yes, my love, I feel fine," she answered.

"I love being at home but I need to get back into town and

tend to the library. If you feel well enough to move around, I should get back to what I was doing before," Emma said softly.

Olyvia leaned toward Emma and patted her hand and said, "My dear sweet little girl. You have grown into such a good woman. I know that it is Seth you need to get back to."

"But, Mama," Emma said.

"Shhh, it is perfectly alright. Being in love is good. If you feel so strongly about it then by all means do it. Don't let me hold you back. I will manage just fine," she replied.

"Are you sure, Mama? I'll stay on longer if you need me to," Emma said.

"If you are happy in your room over the mercantile, then please go there. Do that much for me, it would make me happy," she replied as she placed her hand on Emma's cheek.

"I would like to go back tomorrow, but only if you are alright," Emma said.

"You go and be happy," her mother said with a smile.

Emma sat in the floor at her mother's feet and laid her head upon her legs and said, "I love you, Mama."

Olyvia stroked Emma's hair and returned with, "I love you too."

Chapter Nine

Emma opened her eyes to Toby's smiling face close to hers.

"Good morning, sister," he said.

Emma ruffled his hair and said, "Good morning, little brother."

"Emma's awake, Emma's awake," he shouted as he ran through the house.

Emma's mouth was watering badly from the scent of bacon. She quickly got herself dressed and as she entered the kitchen she licked her lips the scent was so strong.

"Oh, Mama, that smells so yummy," she said.

She ate quickly and helped with the clean up.

"Emma, I would like for you to come sit and talk with me a while," her mother said.

"What's wrong, Mama?" Emma asked.

Olyvia sat two cups of coffee on the table

"Mama, are you sure everything is alright?"' Emma asked.

"Everything is fine. Here come sit with me," her mother said as she patted the seat next to her.

Emma sat down and Olyvia slid a cup of coffee to her.

"Comfortable?" Olyvia asked.

"Yes, Mama, what is wrong?" Emma asked again.

"In May you had your seventeenth birthday this is already July and way past due. When I learned of my gift my mother gave me a family heirloom in honor of our name. She told me to always treasure it and to always preserve our name and our gift. Now that you are a young woman and in love I think it's time for me to pass this family keepsake down to you," Olyvia said as she took a sip of her coffee.

"In love? How do you know that I'm in love?" Emma asked.

"I see the way the two of you look at each other, your eyes sparkle whenever he mentions your name, he listens attentively when you talk. Now that's love," she answered.

As Olyvia stood behind her daughter she reached into her skirt pocket to retrieve the object she was to give her.

Olyvia slipped a necklace around Emma's neck and said, "My mother gave this to me and said to wear it in confidence. I'm giving it to you and some day you will pass on to your daughter because only the females receive the gift and is usually the first born child. Emma, always be true to yourself and be proud of who you are."

"Oh, Mama, it is so beautiful," she replied as she placed her hand over it.

"The heart shape represents love, the letter of course, represents our Fox name, the pattern that frames the heart represents clarity. In the back is a secret area where you can place a piece of fabric with a dab of oil on it and place it in there," Olyvia calmly said and sat down.

"It's beautiful, Mama, I will treasure it always," Emma replied with a smile.

"It suits you just fine," Olyvia said.

"I will never take it off," Emma said.

"Just promise you will take good care of it. It has been in our family for generations and it is very old," Olyvia replied.

"I promise, Mama, as a woman I will always protect our family name," Emma replied softly.

"Oh come here and give your mama a hug," Olyvia said.

"Thank you, Mama, for all that you have given me," Emma whispered into her mothers ear.

Emma sat on the edge of her bed as her feet dangled. She looked around the room in disbelief that she may never see this room again.

"Emma, are you ready?" her father shouted from another room.

"Yes, Papa, I'm coming," she shouted back.

For a brief moment Emma stood in the doorway of her room as she looked back she smiled and shut the door behind her.

"Mama, I love you," Emma said through tear-filled eyes as she embraced her.

"I love you too, my dear sweet daughter," Olyvia said as she swept the small curls from Emma's face.

"I miss you, sister," Toby said as he jumped up and wrapped his arms around her neck and his legs around her waste.

"I miss you too, little brother," she replied as she ruffled his hair.

"You be a good boy for Mama, I only want good reports about you," she said with a smile.

Toby kissed her cheek and whispered in her ear, "I be good boy for you, sister."

"It's time to go, Emma," her father said.

Emma stood Toby on the floor and said, "I know."

Thomas picked up her bag and they headed for the door as Emma turned she blew them both a kiss. Her eyes filled with sadness as she ran back to her mother and laid her head on her shoulder she said, "Oh, Mama, I'm going to miss you so much," as she sobbed.

"It will be alright," Olyvia said as she wiped Emma's tears and kissed her on the forehead.

"You go now be happy," Olyvia said.

"Okay, Mama, but I'm still going to miss you," Emma replied. Olyvia only smiled.

Emma walked to the door and shut it behind her. As she stood on the other side she took a deep breath and climbed up on the wagon.

"You can come home any time you like," Thomas said as not to break his concentration.

"Yes, Papa, I know," Emma replied.

"If he is not good to you, I will make it right," Thomas said in a stern voice.

"I don't think you have anything to worry about, he's a good man. He cares for me," Emma said with a smile at her father's concern.

"You're my daughter and I just want for you to be happy and loved," Thomas said

"I'm happy, Papa," Emma said.

"Whoa!" he said as he stopped the wagon. "That is all I needed to hear," he said.

"I love him," she said as she put her head down, not to disrespect her father.

"Does he love you?" Thomas asked.

"Oh yes, very much," she said with excitement as she lifted her head to look at him.

"Little one, listen to me. I love you and I care for your happiness. When you are happy then I am happy. When you are sad then I am angry and I have to make things right," he said as he shook his fists.

Emma was upset with the way he expressed himself.

"Good thing I ain't got to do that—huh?" he asked with a smile.

"Oh you won't, Papa," she said gleefully.

"Okay then," he said as he snapped the reins and they were once more moving along.

"Thank you, Papa," Emma said.

"For what?" he asked.

"For letting me be myself," she answered as she laid her head upon his shoulder.

Thomas smiled widely.

Seth and his father sat in rocking chairs on the porch as Thomas and Emma pull up in the wagon.

"Whoa!" Thomas said as he stopped and pulled the brake.

Emma smiled happily when she saw Seth as he started to walk toward the wagon.

Thomas looked at Joseph nodded his head once and said, "Butter. I see your working hard as usual."

"Yep, this is the hardest job I do," he replied as they both giggled.

Seth helped Emma down from the wagon and said, "I'll help you with your bag," as he reached in the back to retrieve it.

"Oh no you won't. I'll get it," Thomas said as he swiftly walked around the wagon. He snatched up the bag, offered Emma his arm with a smile and said, "Shall we?"

"You should get that looked at," Thomas replied as the step squeaked.

"Yes, Papa," Emma said.

"Well this is down right pretty. Looks like you have all your needs in one room," Thomas said as he looked around.

"I'm real happy in my little room," Emma said.

"That's what Papa needed to hear," he said with a smile.

There was a silent pause for a brief moment.

"I best be gettin' back before mother sends a posse out for me," Thomas said as he pulled up his britches and snapped his suspenders.

"You come visit now won't you?" Thomas asked as they embraced.

"Yes, Papa, as much as I can," Emma answered.

"Damn dusty road," Thomas said as he wiped his eyes.

Emma stood at the top of the stairs as she watched her father walk down.

"You really should get that fixed," he said as the step squeaked again.

Thomas climbed up on the wagon and waved goodbye to Emma. He pulled the brake, snapped the reins and waved one more time before he pulled away.

She shut the door and threw herself down on the bed. She was so happy to be back in her one room home, but she felt a little downhearted about leaving her family.

As she lay there, her gaze fell upon the cottage painting and thought of the day she and Seth had spent there.

Emma is awakened by a knock at the door. Seth stood with a wide smile as she opened the door.

He stepped in and pulled her close to him and said, "I have missed you terribly."

"I have missed you too," she said as she wiped the sleepy time from her eyes.

"I was sent to fetch you for supper," he said.

"I'll be down shortly," she replied.

"Alright, but don't be long. I'll be waiting for you," he said as he smiled.

"I bet you will be," she said as she smiled back at him.

After supper Seth said, "Let's go for a walk. It's such a beautiful night, I wouldn't want to see it go to waste."

"That sounds nice," she said as she grabbed her shawl and flung it around her shoulders.

The light of the moon brightened their way as they walked arm in arm along the dirt street to the path.

They walked the path for some time and found a comfortable place to sit and relax by the edge of the river.

The moon shimmered on the river as if it were full of tiny diamonds.

They sat in silence on the long green grass, saturating themselves in all the beauty that surrounded them.

"Will it always be like this lovely for us?" Emma asked.

"I think that as long as we have each other it will always be this beautiful wherever we are," he answered as he reached for her hand.

"When we are separated look up to the moon and think of how utterly perfect this moment is. We will never be far apart from one another because our love is strong and can never be broken," he said as he lifted her delicate hand to his mouth and gently kissed it.

He gazed into her eyes and softly said, "I promised you something special tonight. I'm giving you the moon."

Chapter Ten

Two weeks had come to pass and all seemed back to normal. Emma worked at the library when she saw Seth walk in. She was happy to see him

"Can we please talk?" he asked as he sat at the table and pulled out a chair for her.

"What is it, Seth?" she asked with uncertainty.

"There is a important matter we really should discuss," he answered.

"This sounds unpleasant, please tell what it is," she replied.

"I leave to go back to the university in two weeks right" he asked.

"Yes that is right," she answered.

He sandwiched her hand between his and said, "It's changed."

"What? Why?" she asked with anxiety.

"I just received a letter stating that my classes are starting earlier. Earlier than I thought," he answered.

"When do you leave?" she asked reluctantly.

He lowered his head and answered, "In two days."

Emma immediately jumped from her chair and tended to books on the shelves.

"We can get married before I go," he blurted out.

"Get married, what will that solve?" she asked

"How can you ask me that?" he asked angrily.

Seth stood and turned her to face him, he took her hands into his and kneeled down on one leg as he said, "Emma May Appleton, will you do the honor of being my wife?" As he reached into his pocket and laid the object in her palm. He looked into her eyes and retrieved his hand from hers and asked, "Will you please marry me?"

Emma looked down at her hand and there lay a peppermint ball.

She sniffed and smiled through her tears and nodded her head once as she answered, "Yes. Yes, I will marry you."

Seth stood grabbed her hand and headed for the door as he said, "Good I have the wagon ready to go."

Emma stopped and said, "What? Go where? I have a lot to prepare for."

"If we leave right now we can go to Oldenville, get married and be back by tomorrow evening," he said excitedly.

"Seth, I don't know," she said with plenty of reluctance.

He wrapped his arms around her waste and pulled her close to him as he said, "We are in love and we want to get married. What is keeping us from that? Please say you will, please say you will marry me."

He took her face into his hands as he looked into her tear filled eyes and said, "I have loved you since the first time I laid eyes on you. Please come with me now. Let's start our life together. I'm pleading with you."

Emma lowered her head but Seth did not break his gaze.

"Yes," she softly said.

"What I didn't hear you," he said as he lifted her chin with two fingers.

"I said, yes! Yes! Yes! You big ox!" she shouted with a smile.

Seth stood and just stared at her as he wiped the tears from her face and quickly grabbed her hand and said, "Let's go then."

The road to Oldenville was quite long and a little bumpy.

"Are you sure you want to do this" he asked slyly.

"I certainly am," she answered.

"We can turn back you know," he said with a smile.

Emma playfully slapped his arm and said, "Stop that. I'm worried over what my folks will say when they find out."

"Don't tell them. Wait until the time is right, like I did," he said as he became suddenly quiet.

Emma looked at him from the corner of her eye and asked, "Did you tell your folks?"

"Sorta," he answered.

Emma smiled at his childlike behavior, turned her head back toward the road and replied, "This is a long road, how much longer?"

"We will be there before to long, my darling. Why are you getting jitters?" he asked.

"I'm just anxious to see something other than Emerald Springs," she answered.

As they rode along Emma commented on how beautiful the scenery was as she saw a crossroad ahead of them. She began to wiggle around in her seat as they rode into the big city. The sidewalks were busy with people rushing about with packages and tending to children. She smiled widely at all of the activity going on around her.

"Emma, Emma darling, we are here," Seth said.

She was so mesmerized by what she was viewing, she hadn't noticed that Seth had stopped the wagon and stood beside her to help her down. Without a word she climbed down and they walked to a big building that had JUSTICE OF THE PEACE painted in bold black letters over the door.

They paused for a moment, looked at one another, smiled as Seth asked, "Shall we milady?" While he offered her his arm.

"May I help you?" a woman asked.

"Yes ma'am we are lookin' to get married," Seth answered politely.

The woman smiled, turned and said, "Follow me, it's right this way," as she waved her hand at them.

They walked down a long dreary hallway painted in a dull green and walked into a room full of color.

"Timothy these here young'uns would like to get married," she said to a burly man with a thick beard.

He laid his pipe and newspaper down on the table beside him and replied, "They do? Do they?"

As the man stood he towered Seth. He tilted his head upward to look at Timothy. His hands were large and swallowed Seth's as they shook.

"Well you certainly have come to the right place. My name is Timothy Lee and this young little filly is my wife of forty years. Her name is Meagen but you can call her Meg."

"Seth Waters and this young woman is my bride to be, Emma Appleton," Seth replied happily.

Timothy offered his hand to Emma and shook lightly as he said, "Glad to make your acquaintance Miss. Appleton."

Emma smiled and said, "You too, sir."

"Meg, get my book and wind up the phonograph," Timothy said.

Meg scurried away and returned with a small black book with gold edging around the soft pages.

"A pretty girl like you must have a bouquet," Meg replied as she handed Emma a bunch of flowers with twine tied around them and still dripping with water from the vase she had just snatched them from.

"That is very kind of you," Emma said as she accepted the gift.

"Do y'all have rings?" she asked.

"No, ma'am, I'm 'fraid not," Seth answered.

"We can't have a wedding without wedding rings now can we?" Meg replied.

"I reckon not," Seth said, confused.

"Mother," Timothy shouted.

"What?" Meg asked.

"They would like to get married today. Rings ain't important if they're in love," Timothy said.

"Oh fiddlesticks, don't listen to him. He's just an old man who wants to get back to his pipe and newspaper," Meg replied as she hurried away once again.

Meg soon returned with two rings one small and the other larger.

"Now we are ready for a wedding," she said as she handed each of them the appropriate sized ring.

Seth and Emma knew not to deny Meg. They graciously accepted the rings and said, "Thank you."

As they turned Seth said, "We are ready now, sir."

Timothy stared at Meg to see if she had any more to say, she only smiled at him as if she hadn't a care in the world.

The ceremony was short but touching for Seth and Emma. They thanked the older couple for their kindness and hospitality and started their long walk down the hallway.

Timothy and Meg watched, waved and smiled as they walked away and Timothy replied, "That little lady ain't eighteen. Do you realize that?"

Meg said, "Yes I do, I just wonder how long it will take them to realize their wedding rings are from an old pair of earbobs."

"Well you're quite the little vixen, Mrs. Lee," Timothy said as he followed his wife back into the colorful room.

"Yes I know," she said with a smile as she shut the door.

Seth and Emma walked out of the big doorway they had walked through some time before. As they stopped on the top stair Seth looked at Emma and said, "Well, Mrs. Waters what do you say we rent a room for the night?"

"Can we do that?" Emma asked.

"Yes we can. It's too late to ride back to Emerald Springs

tonight and I'm a little tired from the ride here," Seth answered.

"Okay, but where?" Emma asked.

Seth looked to both sides of him and then pointed across the street as he answered, "We will stay there."

Emma's eyes widened with delight.

The sign above the door read OLDENVILLE HOTEL. The building was large in size and had more than one floor.

Emma was excited; she had never stayed in a hotel before.

Seth offered his arm and they crossed the street to walk up the spacious wooden sidewalk. Tall black lights lit their way.

They entered the lobby that was ample in size. The floor was laid in grey marble, a radiant sparkle came from the chandelier that hung with jewels above them. The furniture looked as if it were to pretty to sit on, covered in plush velvet and made of hand-carved wood.

They checked in and received their key and walked up the wide wooden stairwell to their room on the third floor.

Seth unlocked and opened the door, he picked up Emma and carried her in. As he set her down she started to dance in circles around the room.

"Oh, Seth, this is absolutely amazing. I have never seen anything like this before. The bed is so big and high. How will I ever get on it? And look, there's even inside plumbing!" she shouted.

The dark wood of the four poster bed corresponded with the rest of the furniture. A chaste lounge sat in front of the fireplace while a bottle of wine chilled on a nearby table. The candles on the candelabra were lit and set a romantic feel to the room.

Emma opened the french doors that led out to the terrace and a warm breeze met her face.

"The city looks stunning from here. I can almost see Emerald Springs, " she said as she giggled at her own joke.

Seth joined her on the terrace as he lightly rubbed her back and replied, "Why don't you freshen up as I pour the wine?"

"That sounds nice," she said as she kissed him and was quick to use the inside plumbing.

"Are you hungry, my darling?" he asked as he handed her a tall goblet.

"I'm very hungry. Where would we get something to eat at this time of night?" she replied.

Seth walked to a long braided rope that hung from the ceiling and pulled it as he said, "Watch this."

Several minutes later there was a knock at the door. Seth opened it to see a young man as he stood there dressed in a red and gold uniform.

"May I help you, sir?" the young man asked.

"Yes I would like to order two of your finest steaks please, and some biscuits," Seth answered.

"As you wish, sir. Will there be anything else?" he asked.

"Um, could we have some pie to?" Emma asked.

"Yes, ma'am, coming right up," the young man answered. He walked backwards and shut the door as he walked into the hallway.

Shortly afterward their food arrived. They carried a small table and two chairs out to the terrace to eat by candlelight and watch the then sleeping city.

Seth stretched his arms into the air and said, "I'm tired. I think I will go to bed now." As he covered his mouth with his hand to give a fake yawn and ask, "Would you care to join me?"

Emma lifted her hand to him with a smile and said, "Yes. I will."

She stood beside the large bed and allowed her skirt to fall to the floor and began to unfasten her blouse.

Seth undressed himself and stood in his undershorts and then began to help Emma with her blouse.

He slid the straps of her underdress off her shoulders, one at a time as he kissed each one. It fell to the floor exposing her small rounded breasts.

Seth stared in wonderment at her petite body.

He cupped her breasts in his hands and squeezed loosely as he nibbled on each one.

Emma fell back against the bed as Seth leaned his body into hers.

She could feel his eager hardness as it he pressed against her belly.

She lifted her leg and wrapped it around him and he softly ran his hand up her calf to her thigh as he grabbed her behind and pulled her closer to the hardness he had to offer her.

He lifted her onto the bed and kissed her neck as he worked his way down to her nipples and flicked his tongue all around them. He kissed her belly and when he kissed her thick black hair she arched her back and squealed in delight. Seth looked at her and smiled.

She lay there with her eyes closed as she waited for the next sensation.

He teased her with his tongue as he licked all around her wet opening. He was aroused by the moaning sounds she made, he moved his muscular body atop of hers and looked into her eyes as he whispered, "I need you."

Emma could feel his hardness as he lay on her thigh and she moaned with pleasure as he pushed his throbbing manhood inside her eager and wet entrance.

Seth also moaned as he began to slowly slide himself in and out of her warm opening.

Emma wrapped her legs around his waste to pull him deeper inside of her as she gripped her fingers into his back.

He began to move more swiftly as the sweat pored from their bodies.

Their breathing increased with every thrust of his manhood.

Their hearts raced as they touched the tip of climax.

He thrust into her harder and deeper as they both exploded with pleasure and reached the moment of ecstasy.

When all was complete Seth looked into her eyes while he moved the small curls from her face and softly said, "I love you, Mrs. Waters."

"That sounds so perfect," Emma replied.

"Yes it does," he returned.

They lay as though their bodies were meshed within one another. They kissed and caressed until the night took them into early morning light.

The trip back to Emerald Springs was long and hot.

Seth and Emma had gotten a late move on so when they had reached their small town all of the shops were closed for the evening and all was quiet.

As they unhitched the horses Seth said, "Maybe we should wait to tell anyone. I leave for the university tomorrow that will give us enough time to decide how to break the news."

"How do we explain about last night?" Emma asked.

"I've been thinking about that. We rode to Oldenville to get books that I will need and rented two rooms for the night, because it was to late to ride back," Seth answered.

"I hope that will be enough to satisfy everyone," Emma replied.

Before they entered the house they shared a passionate kiss, they took a deep breath and walked in.

"We thought the two of you had gotten lost somewhere," Mr. Butter said as he smiled.

"We rode to Oldenville to buy the books I need for my classes. We didn't mean to worry you," Seth replied as he shook his father's hand.

"We got books," Emma shouted out very quickly.

Seth looked at her with one eye and asked sternly, "I'm all set now ain't I, Emma?"

"Yes," Emma answered calmly.

Mrs. Butter came from the kitchen and asked, "Did you young'uns have a nice trip?"

Seth and Emma looked at her in disbelief as they thought, "How could she know?"

"I'm going to turn in for the night," Seth said as he stretched his arms and yawned.

"Me too," Emma said as she covered her mouth and pretended to yawn herself.

She waved and said, "Good night y'all." And she walked out the door to go to her room upstairs.

Chapter Eleven

Emma was awakened by the hand of her husband. She knew his touch.

"Hi," she said as she opened her eyes.

"Hi," he said as he smiled at her.

"I didn't think I would get to see you," she said as they lay to face each other.

"I'm right here laying next to you," he said as he moved hair from her face.

"Oh, Seth, I will miss you," she said as they wrap up into one another.

"I know, my darling, but it's only for several months," he said as he kissed her forehead and her nose.

She buried her face into his firm chest and could hear his heartbeat as she thought how safe she felt at this moment.

"When I return we will have a get together and announce our marriage. How would that be?" he asked. "Emma, would you like that?" he asked.

He tried to see her face but he knew that she was sleeping. He lay there and held her in his arms until streaks of light peaked through the curtains. Then he gently laid her down on the bed covered her and kissed her forehead as he said, "I love you."

He slowly crept out of bed and slipped on his boots.

He stood at the open door as he looked back at her he smiled, how peaceful she looked as she slept and he thought to himself what a lucky man he was to have her to come home to. As he quietly shut the door behind him.

Emma awoke and rolled to her side as she expected to see Seth lay there. She felt as if someone had laid rocks upon her heart when he was not there.

She sat up as she noticed a piece of folded paper on her night table.

She felt a little queasy at first but it quickly passed.

She opened the paper and began to read.

My darling Emma,

I sit here as I watch you sleep and I realize how truly in love I am with you. I am lucky to have found you. I want to touch you, feel you but I let you sleep. If this is what it will feel like for the next few months then I surely will go mad. Especially when I am this close to you right now. I would go to the ends of the earth just to be next to you. I will be here with you very soon.

I love you my darling,

Seth

Emma started to cry and then she heard a knock at the door.

"Just a moment," she shouted as she tried to wipe the tears from her eyes.

She flung her shawl around her shoulders and opened the door to see her mother.

"Hello, Emma, may I come in?" she asked.

"Oh yes, Mama, come in," Emma answered as she threw her arms around her mother's neck.

"You've gotten married," Olyvia commented.

"Oh, Mama, I love him so much and now he is gone," Emma said as she sat on the bed and covered her face with her hands as she began to cry.

Olyvia put her arm around Emma's shoulder and asked, "Where did he go?"

Emma looked at her mother through her many tears as she sobbed and sniffed, "He went back to the university," she answered in a most pitiful way.

"Is that all," Olyvia replied as she giggled.

"Is that all? He ain't gonna be back 'til December," Emma said, very childlike.

"Emma, listen to what I say. Love is beautiful when shared by two people. But if you don't feel hurt some times, the love won't mean a thing."

"Really?" Emma asked.

"You and Seth will be alright. He will be back soon and you two can begin your lives together. Your young you will learn as you go," she answered as she handed Emma a handkerchief from her pouch.

"Oh, Mama, I don't know what I would do without you," Emma said as she embraced her mother.

"You will be fine, my love," her mother replied.

"You won't tell Papa, will you? And ain't you supposed to be at home taking it easy, why are you out?" Emma asked.

"Don't worry, my love, I won't tell him and don't make fuss. I ain't gonna just sit at home and do nothing. I'm not an old lady yet," her mother replied.

Emma looked at her and they both started to laugh.

Olyvia stood and said, "I must be going now, my love."

Emma stood as she embraced her mother and said, "Thank you, Mama, for helping me to feel better. I love you."

"I love you too," she replied.

Before she walked out of the room Olyvia looked back at Emma as she said, "Take special care of yourself and my granddaughter." She closed the door behind her with a smile on her face.

Emma stood for a moment speechless as if she were in a daze.

She scooped up the letter Seth had wrote her and crawled back into bed. The cottage was embedded in her mind as she drifted off to sleep.

September and October had come to pass. Emma's mother had been correct pertaining to her being with child. There was no one who would understand; no one knew of their marriage.

Emma wrote several letters to Seth but had mentioned nothing of a child.

She thought "It would be an exquisite Christmas gift for her husband."

Christmas was only a week away and Emma had just finished up her shopping. Seth would be coming home soon.

She hurried up the stairs to get her gifts organized before supper.

The step squeaked on the way up and she had had enough, so she decided to investigate. She laid her packages on the desk and looked around for something to detach the board with, when she noticed the letter opener Mrs. Butter had given her.

She wiggled the instrument in between the two woods and began to pry the step loose. The nails squeaked as she grabbed the top layer of wood with her hands and pried it the rest of the way off. She fell back on her behind and slid some when the board broke loose.

She regained her balance and slowly peaked in side the hole she had created.

To her delight she saw a beautiful wooden box. She carefully lifted the box out and set it beside her and attempted to repair the step the best she could.

The step still squeaked but she thought she would take

care of that later. She curiously wanted to discover her newfound treasure.

She shut the door and sat on the edge of her bed. She stared at the box and wondered what could possibly be inside.

She took a deep breath and slowly opened the lid. The first thing that met her eyes was a skeleton key with a silk pink ribbon tied to it. She dangled it in front of her face.

She peaked in the box one more time and saw a blank envelope. She pulled the letter from it and was curious but yet frightened of what it might say.

She unfolded the top of the page and began to read.

My darling daughter,

I write this letter in hopes that you will find it in your heart to understand what I am about to tell you. When I was a young woman about your age, I met a man whom I fell deeply in love with. His name was Ryce Falcon. We had a romance that was exciting, adventurous and full of passion. We were to be married. I found that I was with child and before I could tell my beloved the people in town forced him to leave. He was an Indian and they didn't take to kindly to that. Without any knowledge of his child he left. I was living with my Aunt Candace at the time. She had no choice but to ask me to leave. She had received aggravation and rude comments from the town's people. I had no way of supporting myself and a child so I rented a room above the inn with the little bit of cash from my aunt, until I could afford something different. I decided at one point to use my vision as a means of support. I actually did quite well for a while. A woman came to me about a man. I told her to serve him tea with a certain flower and he would be hers forever. I did not know that she would serve him the wrong flower and it would make him very ill. He never spoke to her again. Rumors flew all over town and the story was twisted when it had finally ended. My explanation for the truth was not wanted. I too was run out of town, on a rainy night. I was pregnant and had nowhere to go. I had suddenly

116

remembered the key my mother given me some years before. It was to a cottage that sat in the middle of a meadow. I had only been there once as a child. I knew that I could find my way back if I had to. I packed as many of my belongings into a bag and I was escorted out of town. Some months later I gave birth to a beautiful baby girl. Yes, my love, that baby was you. We were happy in our little cottage. When you were only three months old, a man sat on his horse at the top of the ridge. He wore a long black coat and a wide rimmed, black hat. He had appeared out of nowhere. Our relationship blossomed immediately and we fell in love. That man was your papa. He loved you as if you were his own child. Please do not be angry with him. One day we packed up moved back into town and bought the farm. We began our lives as a family. The key belongs to you now. I know that you will treat it carefully just as you have our family heirloom. The cottage has been in our family as long as the necklace. There are stories that are told and untold concerning the cottage and its occupants. Be happy, my love. It will all work itself out. Take good care of your daughter she will be a special child.

I love you with all my heart,
Mama

Emma dropped her hands to her lap as the tears streamed down her face. She did not know what she was feeling.

She released her grip of the letter and let it fall. She suddenly jumped up and ran out the door.

Emma rode home as fast as the horse would take her. When she arrived there were several other horses in the yard, also Doc Finley's wagon.

She ran into the house to find Toby as he sat very quiet on a chair with his head lowered.

There were several people standing around chatting and carrying on about all sorts of things.

No one had noticed that she was there.

"What is happening?" she shouted.

Thomas heard Emma's voice and rapidly ran to her as he placed his hands on her shoulder's he said, "It's your mother. I'm afraid that she has gone to heaven." As he lowered his head and began to sob.

"You're lying! I don't believe it! Where is she? I need to see her right now!" she shouted quite loudly.

Emma ran to her mother's room and as she reached the door she walked in slowly to the bed where her mother lay. She had her eyes closed and seemed to be sleeping very peacefully.

Emma sat on the side of the bed as she stroked her mother's hair and the tears fell heavily.

"Oh, Mama, why didn't you tell me? I am not angry and I love you," she said softly.

"She's still warm. I can help her, she's still warm," Emma screamed as she placed her hand on Olyvia's chest.

It began to glow and just at that moment a few of the women burst into the room.

"What is it child?" one of the women shouted. As they looked in disbelief at the sight of Emma's beautiful gift.

"Mama is still warm," Emma replied as she smiled at the women.

"Oh, little girl, what are you doing to your poor dead mother?" one of them asked.

"What is wrong with your hand?" another one asked as she began to back away.

Thomas then entered the room and shouted, "Emma!"

She looked at him and the pain of her loss surfaced and she ran to her father and began to sob uncontrollably as she laid her head on his chest.

"That child is not right," one of the women said.

Emma lifted her head and looked at her father as she said, "I know everything, Papa, and I'm okay."

He smiled and she hid her head again.

"I can't stay here, Papa," she said as she ran out of the house.

She rode swiftly home while she deeply cried.

She walked up the stairs and it squeaked; she didn't know if she should laugh or cry.

She pulled off her dress and boots and crawled into bed.

She fixed her eyes upon the cottage painting and thoughts of her mother entered her mind. She began to sob once again as she absorbed the events of the day.

Some hours later Emma is awakened by a knock at the door as she opened it she saw her father as he stood there with his hat in his hand.

"Hi, Emma," he said.

She wrapped her arms around his neck and began to cry as she said, "Oh, Papa."

He patted her back and said, "It will be alright. I'm here to say goodbye."

Emma looked at him with wide eyes an asked anxiously, "Why? where are you going?"

"Toby and me can't stay here. There is nothing left for us with your mother gone. We are moving to California where it is warm and he can play in the sunshine all year round."

"I'm here, please don't go," Emma pleaded.

He took her hands into his own and said with a smile, "My daughter. You have a life of your own to live now. You will soon raise a family of your own."

"How did you know?" she asked.

"Your mother and me shared many things. I am looking forward to becoming a grandfather. But I must give Toby a better life and make happy, new memories. He is still young and deserves that much," he answered.

"I still don't want you to go," she said.

"Emma, you will be fine, you have a good man that will take care of you and your child," he said.

"Can I say goodbye to Toby?" she asked.

"Well, yes you can," he replied.

Emma grabbed her shawl and slipped on her barn boots.

She walked out to the falling snow and as she reached the bottom of the stairs, she could see Toby's cute little, smiling face peak around the side of the canvas.

He climbed out of the wagon and jumped up on Emma as he wrapped his legs around her waste and said, "Hi, sister."

"Hi, little man," she said with a smile.

"I a boy," Toby sighed.

"Are you a good boy?" she asked slyly.

"Yes, I gonna miss you sister," he said.

"I'm going to miss you to. Remember that we will always have our secret place," she replied.

He nodded his head once and said, "I was waiting for you sister. You weren't there."

"What?" she asked.

"You sent a message a long, long time ago. You weren't there," he answered.

"When you are sad you think of that place and we *will* be there together—okay? Can you do that for me?" she asked.

"I love you, sister. I remember our secret place for a long time," he answered.

"I love you too. Now how about a hug?" she said.

She put Toby back on the ground and faced her father.

"Father Evens is saying a few words over your mother this afternoon. I thought you would like to be there," he sadly said.

"I will go," she replied.

"You are a good daughter. You are *my* daughter and don't you ever forget that," he said firmly.

The tears streaked Emma's cold face as she said, "You are *my* papa."

"I will write when we are settled," he said.

"Okay, Papa," Emma replied.

He reached for her hand as he said, "I love you, you know."

"I love you too," she returned.

They embraced one another and Thomas said, "Now you get back inside before you get chilled to your bones."

He climbed onto the wagon, looked at her and winked.

As they started to ride away Toby peaked out and waved good-bye.

Emma was left standing in the cold of winter all alone as the snow fell upon her.

"STOP!" she shouted.

As the wagon came to a halt Emma ran up to it and leaned on the side as she looked up at Thomas.

"You are a good father," she said as she tried to catch her breath.

Thomas looked down and smiled at her.

He snapped the reins and the wagon began to move again.

Emma stood in the middle of the snow-covered street as she waved to Toby and blew him kisses. She watched until the wagon faded and became nothing but a blur off into the cold and snowy distance ahead.

Chapter Twelve

Emma returned to her room to find that she was all alone, and for the first time in her life she was afraid. Her head was filled with confusion. She lay on her bed in the fetal position and tried to process it all as she cried herself to sleep.

Several hours later she awoke shivering. She only wanted to pull the covers over her head and return back to sleep. She did not want to face what lay before her.

She slowly slid out of bed and placed a few logs on the hot coals as she heated some water.

She washed up the best she could and brushed her hair and let it fall down her back just as her mother liked it.

Emma fashioned herself in her best dress and dabbed on a little lavender oil. She flung her cape around her shoulders.

The box sat on the floor and it caught her eye. She picked it up and sat on the bed and opened it slowly . She reached in and lifted out the dangling key. She untied the ribbon from it and slid it into her cape pocket. She placed the key back in the box and pushed it under the bed.

Emma felt as if she should tell the Butters of her mother's

passing. She walked in and Mr. Butter met her at the door and said, "Emma, we are sorry to hear of your mother's parting."

"Thank you, that means a lot to me," she replied.

Mrs. Butter came from the kitchen and asked, "How are you holding up, dear?" As she took Emma's hands into her own.

"I am coming to terms with it all. But I was afraid that you didn't know," Emma said.

"Oh yes, dear, Doc Finley spoke with us earlier in the day," Mrs. Butter said with a smile.

As Mr. Butter sat in the other room Emma couldn't help but notice how fidgety he had become.

"Come sit for a spell, dear, you look exhausted," Mrs. Butter said as she motioned to Emma.

"Only for a moment I really must be getting to the cemetery soon. Father Evens will be speaking for my mama and I would like to be there," she said as she sat on the sofa.

Mr. Butter sat silently in his chair. Each time he rocked the chair squeaked and Emma watched him very carefully.

"Would you care for some tea, dear? Just to warm you before you go," Mrs. Butter asked.

"No thank you," she answered.

"We received a telegram from Seth this morning," Mrs. Butter commented.

"What did it say?" Emma asked.

As Mrs. Butter began to relay the message the rocking came to a full halt.

"Well it seems there has been a error with his scheduling," Mrs. Butter replied.

"Error? What kind of error?" Emma asked as she began to cry.

Mrs. Butter patted the top of Emma's hand and answered, "Well, dear, it seems he will have to take on an extra class."

Emma suddenly became frantic as she asked, "What does that mean?"

"It means. Well, dear, it means he won't be joining us for Christmas this year," she answered softly.

Emma's eyes filled with sadness as the tears welled up.

"How can he do that to me?" she asked loudly as she stood and walked toward the door.

"Where are you going, my dear?" Mrs. Butter asked.

Emma stopped and softly answered, "I have to bury my mother."

After Emma had left, Mr. Butter shouted, "Amelia!"

"Yes, dear?" Mrs. Butter replied kindly.

"Why didn't you tell her?" Mrs. butter walked away with no reply.

Emma stood outside the door her cheeks rosy red from the cold wind and her body chilled as she gathered her cape closer around her.

She did not like the winter months it seemed as though she could never be warm enough.

She tried to ignore the cold as she started her walk across town.

The wind was harsh and her hair constantly blew in her face. She tied her hair back with the pink ribbon she had slid in her pocket earlier.

Emma reached the entrance to the cemetery and stopped for a moment to gather her thoughts. The bitter cold bit at her bones as she tried to build enough courage to face the fact of saying goodbye to her mother.

As Emma walked to her destination she saw the Father standing there.

"Hello, Emma, I am sorry for your loss," he replied.

"Thank you," she said dryly.

"I realize the cold is almost unbearable so I will speak as quickly as possible," he said as he lowered his head to the small black book he held.

Emma stood in complete silence as she stared at the pine box her mother lay in. As she wondered what she was wearing and if she were warm enough.

Emma had hardly heard a word that the father had spoken.

"As we put to rest the soul of Olyvia June Appleton," Father Evens said.

The next thing Emma heard was, "Amen" he had completed his sermon.

Emma reached back and untied the ribbon in her hair and tossed it to the wind. It began to swirl around until it fell softly onto her mother's casket. At that moment the snow began to fall. Emma tilted her head to the sky as she felt the cold, wet flakes touch her face. She closed her eyes and could hear her mother say, "It will all work itself out, my love."

A smile fell upon her face.

"Emma, would you like for me to say a few more words?" Father Evens asked as he cleared his throat.

"No, Father, that was a lovely service, thank you," she answered.

She laid her hand on top of the pine box as her eyes filled with tears she said, "I love you, Mama."

Emma turned and headed for the entrance as she had gotten closer to the gates she noticed that a crowd of people had gathered just outside of the two pillars.

Why hadn't they come to pay their respects, she had wondered.

Women chattered into each other's ears and pointed their fingers as she walked through the gates.

Emma kept her head high and walked right through the crowd as they parted a path for her.

"She's just like her ma and her grandmother," and "That little girl's hand lit up like fire," were some of the things she heard them say.

The crowd followed her to the bottom of the stairs that led to her room.

She turned swiftly as the bottom of her cape swirled around her ankles and the crowd stepped back and said, "Ooh."

"Why must you say such ugly things? My mother was a good woman and friend to you all. So do not stand there whispering and cackling when my back is turned. Do tell me now while I face you all," Emma shouted.

She stood and waited for more than just silence, as she moved her eyes side to side as she watched for some kind of movement.

"Anyone?" she asked.

There was only the sound of crackling branches some where off in the distance.

She began her walk up the stairs as she had almost reached the top, a rock flew through the air and gave her a hard blow to her back.

She stopped and stood still as the crowd waited for her response.

Emma never looked back and continued up the stairs.

She rushed into her room and slammed the door. As she leaned her back up against it, she pulled the latch down to lock it.

Frightened, she tried to catch her breath.

"Oh baby, don't worry I will protect you," she said as she laid her hand on her belly and felt the baby move for the first time.

She looked down, smiled and rubbed her belly lightly as the baby moved again and she said, "I love you too."

Joseph waved his hand in the air and shouted, "Break it up. The girl just lost her mother. Go home to your families, eat supper, have a nice evening. Just leave her alone."

The crowd had thinned but he could still hear the whispers.

One man asked, "Butter, how can you be taken by her?"

"She is a very nice girl and I happen to like her. Now go home," he simply answered.

"We will be back to take care of this, you just watch and see, Joseph Butter, just watch and see," Ruthie Marie said as she pointed her finger at him.

"Ruthie, quit your bickering and go home to take care of your husband," Joseph said with a sarcastic smile.

"Humph," she said as she turned and walked away.

Mr. Butter picked up the plate he had sat down and headed upward to Emma's room.

Emma was startled by the knock on the door.

"Who is it?" she shouted.

"It's me, Mr. Butter," he answered.

She lifted the latch and invited him in.

"The wife thought you might be hungry," he replied as he handed her the still warm plate.

She sat on the bed to eat as Mr. Butter threw more wood on the fire.

"The wood is low. I will bring you more tomorrow," he said.

"Thank you," she said as she shoved another bite into her mouth.

Mr. Butter pulled up a chair next to the stove and warmed his hands over the top of it.

"Emma, how are you feeling" he asked.

"I'm feeling okay. I'm just a little confused that's all," she replied.

"Don't pay no mind to them," he said as he waved his hand.

"What is wrong with them?" Emma asked.

"Just cackling old crows. Their husbands all do as they are told for fear of getting their eyes pecked out," he answered as they both had a good laugh.

"I'm frightened to see what comes next," she replied.

"I'm sorry that my son can't be here with you Especially now, in your time of need. Just be patient and it will all work itself out," Mr. Butter said with a smile.

"My mama always told me that," Emma replied.

"Was she right?" he asked.

"I never really thought about it. But yes, it did," she answered.

"Your mother was obviously a smart woman to give such good advice," he replied. "Well I best go now before Mrs. Butter thinks I ran away," he said.

"Tell Mrs. Butter thank you for the food," she said as she handed him the empty plate.

He looked at it and to her as he smiled and said, "You take care of yourself."

"I will be fine, " she said.

"You latch this door behind me," he said.

"I will and thank you," she said.

"For what?" he asked.

"For being concerned about me," she answered.

He smiled and walked out the door.

He stood on the outside until he heard the door latch.

Emma rubbed up and down on her arms to warm herself. She placed more wood in the stove. She slid into her nightdress and hurried to get under the blankets on her bed. She moved her feet back and forth to warm the sheets.

As she lay there and gazed at the cottage she could almost smell their sweet scent.

"Emma," a woman's voice called to her from a distance.

"Mama, is that you? I can't see you" Emma said as she tried to focus. From out of nowhere she saw her mother walking toward her. She had the most amazing bright light surround all around her. She wore a light blue dress made of silk and chiffon and it flowed with her as she walked. Her sleeves were long and almost touched the ground. White doves flew all around her. As she approached Emma she could see that her mother's beauty was flawless. "I'm right here my love," her mother said with a smile.

"Oh, Mama, I miss you so much it hurts," Emma said.

"You will survive all of this pain you are feeling. I raised a strong woman." her mother replied and she smiled as a dove landed on her finger.

"What is this place?" Emma asked.

"It's a place only you and I can go. Emma, I have something of quite importance to tell you so please listen to what I'm about to say. There are people that are delusional and they will come to you. You must be brave. They will try to break you down with unpleasant ways and dirty insults. Do not accept their words to be true. Be courageous and it will all work itself out," her mother said with a beautiful smile.

"What people are coming? Why are they coming?" Emma asked.

"You will understand when the time arrives and you will know what to do," she answered. Olyvia touched Emma's face with her limpid hand. She closed her eyes to feel her mother's touch. "I must go now, my love," she said.

Emma opened them as her mother was walking away. "When will I see you again?" Emma asked as the tears streamed down her face.

"Just close your eyes and I will be there," she answered.

"I love you, Mama, and I don't want you to leave me again. I'm all alone. Won't you please stay?" Emma pleaded.

"I love you too, my dear sweet daughter, but I must go for now. We will be together again real soon," she said as she disappeared into the light from whence she came.

"Mama, please don't go. Don't leave me here, come back," Emma pleaded as she wept helplessly.

"Be strong my love," her mother whispered.

Emma was awakened by a loud banging noise outside her door. She pulled the covers around her shoulders and slowly peaked out the door. She only saw the glistening of the beautiful white snow.

She stoked the fire and put a few more logs on it and the heat began to raise.

She sat on the bed as she tried to gather her thoughts and put it all into perspective. The wooden box the letter, her mother's death, the crowd of people and that dream. *What sense did that make?* she thought.

"Oh baby, what is going on in there?" she said as she touched her belly while the baby moved around.

I must think of the baby and try to stay happy, she thought.

It was only four days 'til Christmas and she hadn't bought a thing for her in-laws.

"It might be too soon but maybe if I go shopping I can regain some sanity and distract me from the hurt for a while," she thought.

She dressed herself, grabbed her pouch and threw her cape around her shoulders.

She was fastening the buttons on her cape as she walked down the stairs. She hadn't noticed the crowd of people that had gathered at the bottom. As she fastened the last button she looked up to see them watching her.

She tried to walk through and there was no parting of a path this time.

She was bumped back every time she tried to walk through.

A tall dark man approached her as he made his way through the crowd.

"Emma May Appleton?" he asked.

She nodded once.

He unfolded a paper and began to read:

"We the people of emerald springs do not feel that you are fit to live in our town. As a community we have—"

"Look, she has been marked by the Fox family. She wears the necklace," a woman shouted.

The crowd oohed and aahed as they all began to chatter.

Emma covered the necklace with her hand as she grew confused and began to cry.

"Do y'all mind if I finish?" he shouted.

"As a community we have come together and have made a difficult decision. You must vacate the premises of this town. Effective immediately! We will provide you with time enough to gather up your belongings. Then you must go! We have great

sorrow for the loss of your loved one. But our decision is final. You will be escorted to the edge of town in which we may never see you again. Our deepest comforts are with you.

Signed,

The Community

of

Emerald Springs."

"Not one of you people have a loving soul. As a community y'all are rotten eggs in a new basket. My mother was the kindest woman I had the pleasure of knowing. Ethel, she helped you make your wedding dress. Who helped you, Silvie, when your husband took ill? Ester, who helped you with your gardening and canning every year? She touched all of your lives in one way or another. My brother and I played with your children. So why must me and my family be insulted in this manner? We have done nothing to harm any of you," Emma shouted through her many tears.

"Hurt us, you ask? Your mother drove away my Hank. He was supposed to love me forever, but instead he married another," Ruthie Marie shouted very loudly.

"Your grandmother caused for my house to burn down and I lost all that I owned," an older woman shouted.

The crowd cried out all sorts of obscenities, insults and hurtful comments.

Emma had come to the realization that her mother's message was real.

She turned and walked to the stairs as the crunch of the snow under her feet was all that was heard.

She started to pack things in a bag that she had used on an outing with Seth. The wooden box would not fit in easily but she pushed until she made room for it.

She stood at the door and turned for one last look around.

She wiped her tears that rolled down her face and took a deep breath as she shut the door.

As she walked down the stairs, she could see a man with two horses. He sat on one and held the reins of the other.

"Come along, Emma," the tall man said.

He helped her mount her horse and said, "There are sandwiches and water inside the bag. I am sorry for all that has befallen upon you, and I am sorry for all that you must be feeling right now. Wherever your travels take you, I wish you happiness," he said in a gentle voice.

"Thank you for your kind words, but I know what I must do," Emma replied.

"In which direction do you wish to travel, miss?" the man on the horse asked her.

"I will be traveling north. The direction from which I once came," Emma answered.

"Very well then," the man replied as he snapped the reins and the journey began.

The horses' hooves hit the frozen ground and echoed in the cold silence.

The sidewalks were covered with people as they stood quietly and watched Emma be put on display.

She sat erect with her head held high and her wide tan cape spread out upon her horse.

Her long curly hair fell loose on her back as it was covered with snow.

The whispering and pointed fingers were shot at Emma as she rode by.

"I am a princess in a parade," she told herself.

At the edge of town the man handed Emma the reins and said, "Well, miss. This is where we must part, and may I wish all the luck to you."

"Thank you. I can manage from here," she said.

He tipped his hat to her and turned his horse as he headed back into town.

"Well, baby, it's just you and me," she replied as she rubbed her belly.

She looked to the sky and said, "I do love the snow."

She pulled the hood upon her head and began to ride down the trail.

Chapter Thirteen

The air was cold and began to bite at Emma's face. Her back ached, her legs were numb and her stomach started to grumble sometime back. She wanted to stop and eat a sandwich but she was too cold and eager to get to her destination.

The pains in her stomach were getting stronger, she stopped for a moment to hold her stomach and thought, "It ain't time yet; maybe it's just from hunger."

She faintly saw a hill as the snow fell and had hoped there would be a valley below it. She was thankful for the full moon to help brighten her way.

She stopped at the top of the ridge and stared at the snow that had not been disturbed and how beautiful it was as the shone upon it and said, "I'm home."

The snow was deep and the horse could not walk it with a rider. Emma felt sympathy and dismounted as she led her horse through the snow. She thought that Lady did quite well for having a wounded leg at one time.

As she approached the front of the house she removed her

bags and laid them on the ground, as close as she could get to the door. She led Lady inside the lean-to on the side of the house. To her surprise, oats and straw had already been prepared for her. She made the horse comfortable and headed for the house.

Emma dug around in her bag and retrieved the key her mother gave to her. She brought it to her face and stared at it; she took a deep breath and slid it into the keyhole. She stood and procrastinated whether to turn it or not. It was so bitterly cold and she was hungry. She turned the key slowly to the right and she heard it click. With her other hand she turned the knob and the door opened. She retrieved the key from the lock and tucked inside her pocket. The door creaked as she pushed it open, with every step she took to enter her little cottage.

Once inside she smiled and placed her hand on her belly as she said, "I think we are going to like it here." She grabbed her bags and tossed them inside.

She managed to find a lantern and lit it. The room was brightened and she noticed a folded paper on the table. She pulled out a chair and sat down to read it.

My darling daughter,
I knew you would come. Have you forgotten my gift of vision? This is your birth place and this is where you will birth your daughter. Be strong my love and it will all work itself out. Remember to look under the box.
I love you with all my heart,
Mama

The tears rolled down her face as she struggled to pick up her bag. She shook it vigorously as the contents fell to the floor and the wooden box made a giant thud as it hit. She picked it up and sat it on her lap and stared at it as she contemplated on whether to look or not. With a hand on either side, she turned it over to reveal an envelope taped in place. She unfastened it, careful not to tear anything and held it in her hand. She opened the envelope and slid out what was inside as she turned it over and revealed this object she began to cry. It was a family photograph.

"This was the only one we had because it was all that Papa could afford," she said. Emma became distraught and again the feeling of being alone and frightened returned to her. Soon she came to realize all was well.

She touched her tummy and said, "This is your grandma," as she held the picture to her belly, "and she says that you are a girl."

Emma dried her eyes and decided to investigate a bit.

She sat in the dining area and could see the picture window; it had a cushioned seat. She Especially liked this because it overlooked the meadow and the moon's light shone right in. The livingroom area had a plump oversized sofa with pale green leaves and pink roses as its pattern. The fireplace was made of stones and had two wingback chairs faced it with a large round rug under them both. The floors were made wood so she knew that the rug would be useful. On another wall was a large bookcase filled with all sorts of books.

She felt her stomach grumble and sat at the dining table as she dug in the bag for the sandwiches.

She stared at the kitchen as she ate. It was the prettiest little kitchen she ever laid eyes on.

A big thick wooden counter with shelves beneath it and red and white gingham fabric hung down as a covering. There was big iron sink with a pump for water. The same fabric hung on the window over the sink. She also had her own stove and ice box.

Emma ate one sandwich very quickly, and when finished she built a fire to get warm and grabbed the other sandwich and sat on the window seat.

She sat and became mesmerized as she watched the snow fall. She stared up at the moon and remembered the night her and Seth sat by the water. Her finger tips touched the wet glass as she said, "Oh, Seth I love you, won't you please come to me?" The moisture began to trickle as she made a wish. She kissed her palm and blew it to the moon, "He will get my message, I know he will," she said as she yawned.

She picked up the lantern and headed for the bedroom. As she walked in she noticed a rocking cradle on the other side of the room but she was too tired to investigate tonight.

She slid in between the cold sheets but she was too tired to notice, immediately she was asleep.

Months had passed since Emma first arrived at the cottage. It was now the month of April.

The flowers had budded and the trees had begun to turn green.

Emma often sat under the tree she and Seth had first made love as she rubbed her belly. She read and talked to the baby. Emma smiled at the fact that her belly had swollen the same as Mama's when she had carried Toby. Emma was enjoying her pregnancy.

It was an unusually warm day as Emma worked in her garden. The sun was beating down on her and she was feeling a little uncomfortable. She wiped her forehead with the back of her gloved hand and just as she stood to get a taste of water, she felt pressure in her belly and a heavy rush between her legs. She doubled over as the pain worsened.

Her belly slowly became hardened and she doubled over in pain once again. As the painful twinges tapered off she held her belly and walked softly into the house.

As she passed through the house she picked up a pitcher of water from the dining table that she had set there earlier in the day. She went to her bedroom, set the pitcher on her bed side table and stripped of her clothes. She threw the heavy covers to one side of the bed and gently lay herself down. She grabbed a cloth from the table beside her bed and wet it to lay on her face. She closed her eyes to rest as the pain subsided.

Several minutes later her belly hardened and the constricting pain again returned and was more unbearable than the last. It slowly faded away as she began to breathe normally again.

Hours passed as the pain repeatedly commenced and subsided. It was now time as she had reached the moment to give birth.

She clenched the bars of the headboard as the sweat dripped from her body and she was getting weak, she took a deep breath and pushed, she pushed as hard as she could.

She felt the baby's head as it slid out.

Crying, she grasped her knees and pulled them up as far as she could. She took another deep breath and began to push again. This time harder and longer.

Emma screamed in delight as the pressure of the pain subsided and the baby lay on the bed crying. She released her legs, setting one on each side of the baby.

Emma sobbed with happiness as she cradled the baby in her arms, smiled and said, "Finally we meet."

She wrapped the tiny wrinkled hand around her finger and kissed it.

She kissed the head of red curly hair and said, "Welcome home, my sweet Abigail."

Emma reached for a blanket to wrap the baby in and laid her on her chest and said, "Grandma was right after all."

She kissed her one more time and said, "I love you, Abigail April Waters," as they both fell fast asleep.

Some time had passed and now it was the month of June.

Emma and her new baby were adjusting quite well to one another. The bond between them had grown.

The warm days kept them outdoors as they enjoyed the sun, the birds, the flowers, and Emma told Abby of how she would learn to chase butterflies.

They sat under the maple tree while Emma told tales of faraway places.

Abby did not understand a word but she smiled at her mother and that made Emma's heart happy.

The streets were empty and it had started to rain as Seth entered into town late that evening.

He anticipated being with his bride and to find out why she had quit writing to him so long ago.

He quickly tended to his horse as the rain came down harder.

He ran up the stairs as he skipped steps as he went. He opened the door quietly as not to disturb Emma. He tiptoed to the side of the bed and swiftly undressed himself.

The room was chilled, so why were the blankets at the end of the bed, he thought.

He rolled to the other side of the bed to touch his wife but she was not there. He felt around the whole bed to find it was empty.

He jumped quickly and lit the lantern.

Emma was nowhere in the room.

He got dressed and searched around for some clue of where she might be.

He picked up her nightdress from the floor and sat on the bed. He ran his fingers over the feminine ruffle and brought it to his face to touch his cheek with it. He closed his eyes and smelled her scent of lavender.

He fell back on the bed as he buried his face in her nightdress and began to cry and after some time he fell asleep.

The lightning that cracked outdoors awakened Seth from his sleep.

He jumped from the bed and ran through the door into the pouring rain.

The echoing sound of the rain could be heard as it hit the ground.

Seth stood in the street as the rain fell upon him. His clothes clung to his body, his hair drenched with water as it hung in his face.

He raised his arms to the sky and tilted his head back as he began to scream very loudly, "EMMA! WHERE ARE YOU?"

He sobbed uncontrollably as he began to turn in circles and shouted again, "EMMA!"

He became weak at the knees and fell to the ground as he held his hands to his face.

The wet dirt slapped Seth in the face as he smashed his fist into the mud that surrounded him.

"She got run out of town, son," his father said as he appeared from around the corner of the building.

"What?" Seth asked as he looked up with reddened eyes.

Seth stood and walked to his father and asked, "Who would do such a thing?"

"Something about her hand on fire. It happened right after she buried her mother," he answered.

"Why did you not write of this to me? How could you let them do that to her?" Seth asked angrily as he grabbed his fathers shoulders.

Joseph stood as not to move a muscle and answered, "I could not stop them."

"Her mother died? She must be completely alone," he replied as he released his grip.

Tears fell from Seth's eyes as he looked at his father and raised his voice as he asked, "Where did she go, old man?"

"She went north. That's all I know," he answered.

"North?" Seth asked anxiously.

"Yes," he answered.

"I gotta go," Seth replied as he turned to run. "Thanks, Pop, I love you," Seth said as he returned to embrace his father and kissed him on the cheek.

"Find her, son," Joseph replied as Seth turned to leave.

"I will, Pop," Seth replied and smiled.

Seth quickly prepared himself for the journey he was about to embark upon.

His eye caught the painting of the cottage, as he walked closer to it he noticed the rock he gave Emma, as it sat on the easel. He picked it up and smiled as he tucked it into his bag.

The sun was shining and it was a perfect day to be outdoors.

Emma and Abby sat under a tree as they played.

As Emma looked up and noticed a man at the top of the hill. He was dressed in a long black coat and a wide black hat.

"Your daddy is here," she said as she stood.

He rode slowly down the hill to the path. He jumped from his horse, never to break his gaze of Emma, and he began to walk the path, as he led his horse behind him.

Emma began to walk toward the man careful not to break her gaze upon him.

She could see his face almost clearly. She walked slowly and then she picked up her skirt tail and began to run toward him

She smiled through the tears that rolled down her face.

Seth smiled and dropped the reins. As Emma ran to him, she slammed her body into his and wrapped her arms around his neck.

He slid his arms around her waste and twirled her in the air.

They share a passionate kiss.

With their faces just inches apart Emma looked into his eyes as hers dripped with tears and said, "I knew you would find me." Emma took him by the hand and said, "I have someone I would like for you to meet."

"What? Who?" he asked.

Emma only smiled.

As they reached the tree where Abby lay, she looked up at them and giggled.

Emma reached down to get her and kissed her baby.

"This is Abby," she said.

"Abby?" he asked.

Emma looked at him through a tearful smile and said, "Abby, this is your daddy."

"I have a daughter?" he asked happily.

"Abigail April Waters," Emma replied.

"Can I hold her?" he asked.

Seth smiled at Abby and said, "Hello, pretty girl, I'm sorry it took me so long to get here. But I'm your daddy." Abby touched his cheek with her pudgy little hand and Seth began to cry.

"We made something that no one will ever be able to take from us. Just as no one will ever take our love, with our love we have Abby. We win all around," Emma replied.

"She's perfect," Seth said.

Abby put her fingers in his mouth, looked at him and smiled as she laid her head down on his shoulder.

"I think she needs to rest. Let's go inside and I can tell you of all that you have missed," Emma said.

They walked the path to the cottage as they smiled constantly at one another.

As they stopped at the door Seth said, "I promise to always make you happy and never to leave again."

Emma touched his cheek softly and replied, "I know."

They shared a passionate kiss and the door shut behind them.

Several months later Abby was lying in her cradle for an afternoon nap. Emma covered and kissed her as she said, "I love you, my little princess." Emma gave the cradle a little push and blew her a kiss. She walked out of the room and shut the door behind her. The cradle slowly rocked back and forth as Abby lay inside. Abby giggled as a teddy bear that sat on a shelf close to her cradle fell in. Or did it?

THE END?

Printed in the United States
104470LV00002B/7-12/A

Printed in the United States
104470LV00002B/7-12/A

9 781424 196708